CHASING DREAMS

Aaron Jennings

For Theresa, my beautiful wife and soul mate

Acknowledgements

Many thanks to my parents, Theresa, Pete Repka, Tom Wyld, Sarah Jones, Lisa Frood, Neil Hammond, Bob Wallace and Heidi Frith for all your ideas, skills and help along the way.

One

My best friend Ben had come up with the idea of going away to Newquay for a weekend in August. Formerly a fishing village, Newquay was now a town notorious for the four B's - beaches, bars and babes in bikinis. We had a month before we were due to head back to school for our final year and I welcomed the distraction from the thoughts of university and work that had been dominating our lives over the past few months.

So there we were, two horny seventeen-year-olds on our first big trip away from home without our parents, squeezed into a tiny two-carriage train with hundreds of others, all headed for the beaches and bars. Although we were both underage, Ben had the distinct advantage when it came to getting served alcohol by looking a little older than he was, with a stocky six-foot frame and more hair sprouting from his chin than on his head. I, on the other hand, was often mistaken for fifteen, but what I lacked in height and stubble, I more than made up for with boyish good looks and immaculately styled hair. Not only that, my clothes were more grunge than hooligan which in my mind made me the front-runner for pulling during the weekend.

Stepping off the crowded train and onto the platform I began to feel in over my head. Everyone was rushing past with purpose and the sight of a small palm tree made the town feel even more distant from home, as if we'd arrived in a tropical version of England. For a brief moment I considered jumping back on the train and writing off the weekend as a bad idea, but Ben had already plodded on ahead and was making a beeline for the taxi rank. Sucking in my nerves I followed his lead, hoping he knew what he was doing.

As the car slowly made its way towards the town, stopping a few times as people spilled off the pavements and onto the roads, I was blown away by the sheer number of people around. Rolling down my window to take in the warm breeze and check out at some of the beautiful bodies we were passing, I began to relax and catching Ben's eye, I couldn't help but smile.

By the time we arrived at the hostel, I felt I had a rough feel for the town and we'd had our first glimpse of the sparkling sea, a rare sight for landlocked teenagers. Climbing the dozen or so stairs to the

1

hostel entrance was a nerve racking experience comparable to a first day of school. Scattered about on the steps and the small porch area were eight guys in their mid-twenties, all sixteen eyes weighing us up as though we were lost. They were all deeply tanned and dressed in a uniform of baggy boardshorts, unkempt hair and scraggly beards. Hesitating for a moment, I threw a second glance at the building sign, it was definitely our place, welcome or not.

'What's up bru?' one of the guys asked Ben. He had shoulder length blond dreadlocks and a foreign accent.

'Uh...where's the reception?' Ben asked him, with nerves coming through his voice.

'Sorry, we're already full up bru,' he said bluntly to Ben, shooting me a look too, just to make sure we understood.

'That's okay we've already booked. Should be under Ben and Matt,' Ben replied, finding some confidence.

'Oh... Oh okay. Follow me,' the dreadlocked receptionist said, smiling for the first time. 'You're in room 6, I'll just grab your keys,' he added, disappearing into the building and leaving us alone with the other guys, who had turned their attentions away from us. As we waited for the receptionist to come back, every second felt like an hour and although the guys were now ignoring us, I sensed that the slightest move or sound would bring their intimidating stares back onto us or, worse, they might cancel our booking, force us away, and we'd be stranded in a strange town with nowhere to stay.

Entering the building, I was blown away with just how cool it looked. All around, the walls were covered in surf posters. To the left was a small room with a TV and pool table, to the right a kitchen and straight ahead past the stairs, a big lounge with half a dozen comfy sofas and another big screen TV. Turning back and climbing the stairs to the rooms, I already felt at home and felt confident enough to try and make small talk with the receptionist. As he opened the door to our room, I seized the chance to break the ice.

'Where in Australia are you from?' I asked but as the words left my mouth, I realised I was saying something wrong. His smile evaporated and was replaced by a snarl, while his eyes frosted over.

'I'm from *South Africa* bru,' he replied, one hand still holding onto the door, barring our entry. Again, time slowed down as I tried to think of something I could say to fix the situation, as he too seemed to be thinking things through in his own mind. Finally, after a couple of seconds of deadlock, he let go of the door, handed Ben the keys and walked away. Stepping inside I couldn't believe I'd nearly blown it for us both in just minutes of arriving but Ben seemed blissfully unaware just how close we'd come to heading home so soon.

Looking around our dormitory, I was comforted to see it decorated just like an average teenager's room with posters on the walls and the floor covered in clothes and magazines. Although I knew one or all of our roommates could be from the pack downstairs, I was feeling comforted both by Ben's blissful demeanour and the fact that we now had the keys. We were in.

Already late in the afternoon, we'd so far spent the whole day on trains or waiting for trains and all we wanted to do was hit the beach. While I waited for Ben to get changed out of his jeans and into a pair of shorts, I walked over to the window and watched a constant stream of people walk past, all headed for the beach.

'Are you not getting changed?' Ben asked me.

'Nah, I'm good. Hurry up though mate,' I answered. Already wearing navy baggy shorts and a worn out band t-shirt, which was my standard ensemble in the summer months, I thought back to the guys on the steps, pleased that my own dress sense wasn't too distant.

'If only we were a year older Matt,' Ben commented to me as we walked past a group of stunning older girls, not a single one noticing our existence.

'We're old enough mate, I mean we're here, no?'

'Yeah, but you look about twelve and although I may look eighteen or nineteen...' he said stroking the hair that proudly poked out of his chin. '...I still feel young here; I haven't seen a single honey our age yet. Have you?' he asked.

'Well no, but we've only been here five minutes. Wait until we get down the beach and I guarantee it'll be heaven.'

'Yeah, but still, your face of bum fluff and freckles reflects poorly on me and causes people to question my age for being with you, which is going to stop me pulling to my potential,' Ben said half-jokingly as he lit up a cigarette. I knew there was an element of truth in it so I hit back.

'Ben, buddy, down here I'd say that being dressed like a yob with your shaven head, football shirt and that big gold hoop in your ear, the only thing you'll be pulling is your own dick. Look around you; the surfer image is the way forwards here, either that or the grunge look, which is of course what I'm going for,' I said watching him fiddle with his earring as he considered my words.

3

'Oh! Like you know what women want. How many girlfriends have you had? Was it one or possibly two?'

'Oh, piss off, as though you're a Casanova,' I said distractedly, as a couple of guys with surfboards under their arms brushed past us and jogged off in the direction of the beach, instantly turning the heads of some passing women.

The sand was jam-packed with families staking their plots with windbreakers, groups of lads playing frisbee and football, sunburnt idiots all brandishing a worrying shade of red and of course, there were the girls. Some wore vests and skimpy skirts but even more were in bikinis and we were in paradise.

It took me no time at all to assess that the best of the beauties were either in groups or with guys, many of whom had surfboards and bodyboards beside them on the sand. Both situations made them impossible to approach.

'Ben, we should go surfing tomorrow,' I said, picturing myself with a board under one arm and a bikini-clad babe on the other.

'Nah, I don't know mate. The water looks pretty cold. Look at that guy getting out over there, he's got a wetsuit on and he still looks frozen. I reckon we should just chill on the beach and watch the girls go by,' he said, grimacing at the thought of the cold Atlantic Ocean.

'Come on, I've always wanted to try it. It'll be fun,'

'By all means do it, but I'm not going anywhere near the icy polluted water,' he said, shrugging off the idea. Although surfing had always appealed to me, there was no way I was going to do it alone, so I decided I'd have to do the next best thing and get the look.

That night we set out into town early with hopes that we'd be at the pubs before the bouncers pitched up and then, with alcohol induced confidence, we'd be able to breeze past the angry looking doormen right into the nightclubs. It was a strategy that couldn't fail, not after months of eager anticipation and planning, and the smart shirts we'd both bought for the occasion.

Our worst fears quickly became reality when it became evident that our untested fake IDs were worthless. The pubs we tried wouldn't serve us any drinks and the bouncers looked too intimidating to even approach. So we really didn't have any other option but to head on back to the hostel. It was just past eight-thirty, when we made our sober walk back through the town centre. The devastating reality of a party-less weekend in a party town was beginning to flood in, while all

4

around us everybody else was full of intoxicating laughter and happiness.

The hostel was almost deserted; a couple were sprawled out on a couch in the lounge watching an old American sitcom but the smaller poolroom was empty. We didn't fancy the idea of spending the night watching TV in the lounge, as we could have stayed at home to do that, so we decided to spend a portion of our beer money playing pool and drinking coke. While Ben racked the balls, a man in his early fifties came in and walked behind the hostel bar. Barefoot, wearing shorts and a tatty t-shirt, with a greying beard, his short blond hair was beginning to recede.

'Hey guys, how you doing?' the man asked, his voice slow and easy with a strong Cornish accent.

'Yeah, not bad thanks,' I answered, walking over to the counter to speak with him.

'You boys not going out into town tonight?' he asked.

'Nah, we tried but we couldn't get served. I thought this town was supposed to be slack on underage drinking,' I said, feeling defeated but eyeing up a clear fridge behind him with a few bottles of beer in.

'It is slack *if* you've got breasts, or if you at least look old enough,' he smiled at me. 'But if you want a beer you can get one here, I'll serve you.'

'*Really*? Cool...Okay... Thanks,' I answered, a little shocked and surprised at his offer, especially as I'd just told him we were underage.

Our saviour for the night turned out to be Craig, the owner of the hostel. He joined us at the pool table and put a surf video on the big screen TV that sat in a corner of the room. In the video the water looked warm and tropical, no one wore wetsuits, the sun was always shinning and on the land towering palm trees bordered the beaches just metres away from the waves. Craig pointed out some of the various surf spots and countries shown in the videos, some of which he had visited over the past couple of decades, as I tried to absorb the magnificent images flicking in front of us. Now married with two small children, he and his French wife intended to sell the hostel and move to Tahiti in an effort to retire early and surf some of the world's best waves. The lifestyle he lived sounded more like a fantasy, something way out of reach for mere mortals like Ben or myself, but, nevertheless, I couldn't help but feel inspired towards the impossible.

Despite the beers we didn't get drunk, and unsurprisingly, nor did we meet any single young ladies that first night, but we did go to

5

bed safe in the knowledge that we could get more beer for the Saturday night. Spending our first night in the dorm room was a strange experience and one of very little sleep. The warm August night air was causing me to sweat inside my sleeping bag but I felt that I couldn't abandon it in a room full of strangers.

We still hadn't met any of our roommates and my first glimpse came when one came in and turned the light on, made a lot of noise, and then disappeared again leaving the room still illuminated. I waited a minute to see if he'd return before reluctantly sliding down from my top bunk and hopping over in my sleeping bag to turn it off. Frustratingly, Ben was in reaching distance of the switch but was fast asleep, his snoring breaking the silence of the room. I was still wide awake as the others filtered in over the next hour or two, each one turning the light on and seemingly making as much noise as they could.

The room was free of bodies and swamped with sunlight through the open curtains when I woke up the following morning. Pulling on my shorts and t-shirt I opted to leave my trainers behind and go barefoot for the first time since I was a child, but as so many others did in Newquay. Downstairs was also deserted, although the TV was still on, blaring away. Walking outside into the bright sunlight, I could see the sun worshipers were already ascending for another day at the beach. Only one person was out on the porch, a guy in his mid-twenties, barechested with a dripping wetsuit zipped down to his waist, short scruffy brown hair and a few days worth of dark stubble. He was absorbed in his own world, tending to a surfboard, rubbing it down with sand paper and cursing. I decided it was best not to disturb him, so I walked over to the steps and sat down with my back to the stranger, figuring Ben would soon be back from wherever he had gone.

'Have you been out yet?' the guy called out, although he was still looking down at his board. I took a couple of quick glances around to see to whom he was talking but there was nobody else in sight.
'Out where?' I nervously asked him, unsure whether he was talking to me.
'Out, out. You know, the ocean,' he replied, nodding his head in the direction of the beach. 'It's going off out there, the waves are pumping... I'd still be in if I hadn't dinged my board on my first wave this morning,' he answered, looking up at me for the first time.

6

'*No*... I can't surf... but I want to learn,' I said, wondering if my reply was cool enough or if I should have come up with a better reason for not having *gone out*.

'Well you're in a good place to start.'

'Maybe next time, I don't really have the money or spare hours this weekend,' I lied, turning around to properly face him for a better conversation.

'That's a shame, you from London?'

'Near there yeah, are you from Newquay?' I asked him, although I felt I could detect a slight Australian accent but I didn't want to offend another South African, or anyone else for that matter.

'Nah, I'm from London,' he replied, before extending his hand out. 'My name's Noodle.'

'Matt,' I said, shaking his firm grip.

'So let me guess Matt, you're just here for the babes, beer and beach?' he smiled.

'That *was* the plan. But I couldn't get into any clubs or pubs yesterday, so that's all kind of gone out the window.'

'Really? I'd have thought you'd get served with no problems here,' he said before turning his attention back to his surfboard, eyeing up his handiwork.

'Well, maybe if I at least looked my age I would,' I responded.

'Or had breasts,' he added.

As I waited around for Ben to return, I carried on chatting with Noodle while I watched him repair his surfboard. He'd moved down to Newquay two years earlier after he'd fulfilled a childhood dream and spent a weekend learning to surf. That brief escape from the city had been more inspirational than he'd hoped and after a few months back in London, he'd quit his well-paid job with a computer firm and opted to leave the daily stresses of the city behind him. These days he lived a simple life as a barman in one of the nightclubs, which left his days free to enjoy the summer. Best of all, he only did that from April until September every year and spent the winter months travelling around the world enjoying an endless summer, surfing and picking up odd pieces of work every so often to boost his money.

It was while Noodle explained this to me that I noticed a look in his eyes. It was one of contentment and satisfaction, as though he knew a wonderful secret and was sharing it with me. In some respects it sounded a little like Craig's plan and certainly a million miles away from the office rat he'd once been. Back home I was gearing up for my

7

last year of school and had been trying to figure out which way my own life should go. The options were threefold, I could stay in education and go to university, head out into the real world and get a job, or take a gap year and travel. The frontrunner by a clear mile was the gap year but none of my friends were interested in backpacking and it wasn't something I felt confident to do alone. In a distant second was university but only because it meant delaying the inevitable life of work and drudgery. One thing was for sure though, I didn't want to end up like my older sister Rachel, sat in front of a computer in a stuffy office for the rest of my life.

Our dad had always hated his job but when he was young he felt too insecure, or too financially dependent, to change jobs and really do what he wanted with his life. Now, years on, he felt stuck, too old to change but too young to retire. Hardly surprising, he'd always told us to find a job we liked, one that would make us happy and just go for it. Rachel had ignored his advice and opted for another path, choosing money over freedom and perhaps with it, a form of happiness. With workdays full of stress and boredom, her weekends are crammed with shopping and clubbing. So with her high income, she's managed to surround herself with material luxuries but gets high as a kite every weekend to escape her bittersweet reality.

Rachel had shown me a lifestyle that had no appeal whatsoever. Now it was up to me to find something that suited *me*. Noodle, it seemed, had the right idea, or at least the right idea for *him*. I realised his lifestyle wasn't everyone's cup of tea, but I could certainly see the attraction. With his life of ease it looked like the ocean created his biggest concerns, how big will the surf be? What's the tide doing? Wind? And so forth. He skateboarded five minutes down a hill to work and strolled back through the sleeping town at night. Such a difference to his old work journey, where he'd stood huddled among hundreds on a packed and overheated tube for two hours each day, commuting around the busy capital, only to wake up and do it all again the next morning. Something that equated to almost five hundred hours a year, wasted, standing shoulder to shoulder with strangers on trains in uncomfortable silence and dreading the hours at work ahead. Now he wore shorts, a t-shirt and trainers to work and only ever shaved when he could be bothered. His was a world that depended on money but wasn't dominated by it and one that I couldn't help but tell Ben all about when he finally showed up a little while after Noodle had dashed off back into the surf, with his fixed board.

Making our way from the hostel, we headed into the town centre for some late breakfast before visiting the many surf shops. The clothes were all expensive so Ben decided to keep his wallet closed. I, on the other hand, was prepared to hand over my cash to achieve the surfer look, which in my mind was going to help me get laid.

Coming out of a surf shop, bags in hand, a familiar face was walking in and much to my pleasure, I got a smile of recognition.
'Hey Matt, you found your friend then?' Noodle said, looking at Ben.
'Yeah man. Noodle this is Ben, Ben... Noodle,' I watched as they nodded at one another.
'You know, I was thinking about you guys earlier, there's a party going on down the beach tonight and seeing as you can't get into any of the clubs I figured you might want to go.'
'A beach party, *alright*,' Ben said with enthusiasm.
'Where abouts? I mean which beach?' I asked.
'Fistral, you know the main one. Just head down there tonight and look for a fire, you won't miss it. I'm not working tonight so I'll be down there anyhow, so I'll see you guys there.'
'Alright, cool,' I said and watched him go.
'Shit mate, a fucking *beach* party. How cool is that? There are *always* keen sexy women at those things,' Ben stated as we carried on our journey.
'How do *you* know that?'
'Hollywood told me so,' Ben said with excitement.
'Wow, must be true then,' I quipped with sarcasm, though secretly hoping he was right.

The wooden pallet looked lost amid the growing flames. I looked down and inspected my new clothes in the orange glow of the fire, hoping that my beanie, baggy jeans and hooded top were giving me an undisputed place in the circle of unfamiliar faces. We'd been a little unsure about what to do when we had approached and realised that Noodle wasn't present but as we stood around, thinking about heading back, one of the girls in the circle called us over and made some space for us.

Ben and I had each brought a couple of bottles of beer from the hostel with us but the ten minute walk had resulted in only a few remaining mouthfuls, so when a nudge on my left side drew my attention away from the commotion of thoughts in my mind and

9

towards a hand extending from the darkness offering a joint, I welcomed the offer. I held it for a moment, reflecting on the sweet smell I was so used to masking and hiding from the suspicions of parents and teachers. This time though, sat on a beach and miles from authority, I was free to enjoy it.

Drawing hard on the crackling reefer, I noticed the most beautiful woman I'd even seen sat straight across the fire from me. Flowing brown curls and a smile that could sell a million toothbrushes, she was rhythmically pounding on a small wooden drum between her legs. The pulsation from the beat was hypnotising and for a moment, I was lost staring at her. Taking another drag of the joint, I felt a little paranoid about the rules of etiquette with regards to how much to smoke, not even knowing whose joint it was, but simply aware that it wasn't all for me. Suddenly feeling self conscious, I quickly passed the glowing butt to Ben.

As I watched from afar, my dream girl stopped playing the drum and passed it to a guy who was a metre or so to her right. To her left was a less attractive girl with short blonde hair and a big nose ring. Examining the circle I sussed out that she didn't seem to be with any of the guys, which left the road clear for myself, even though she was clearly at least five or six years older than me and way out of my league. Glancing around the circle of flickering faces, her gaze stretched across and over the flames and locked onto my own, throwing me a smile that showed her recognition of my stare, obviously knowing that my own eyes had been chasing hers through the flames. It was an understanding smile that one associates with any beautiful woman who knows she's beautiful but one that told me I hadn't a chance in hell.

For a minute I watched the flames as they ate away at the pallet but it wasn't long before my gaze moved away, past the sparks sailing into the black sky and again towards the girl. She was focused on the fire, nodding in time with the drum that was now accompanied by a didgeridoo and the constant rhythmic crashing of waves not so far behind me. Closing my eyes I felt like I was in another country sitting on a beach far away and suddenly the realisation hit me, I could be.

A little while later a figure walked out of the darkness to the left, his head shrouded in a dark hood, an orange glow briefly illuminating from the black space where his features were hidden. A stab of jealousy washed in my gut as he sat down next to my girl and gave her a kiss. He wore a hooded sweater with the word *mellow* written across it in big white letters. As he pulled the hood down, I realised with surprise that this rival for my love was none other than Noodle, who with glazed eyes caught my stare. Offering me a wide smile and a nod of recognition, in an instant my jealousy washed away as I returned his friendly nod. A part of me felt I should hate this prick who had *my* girl but he had seemed to be a genuinely nice guy. In fact, Noodle was the sort of guy I was beginning to realise I wanted to be and what's more, he had the kind of girlfriend I dreamt about.

As my jealousy did a one-eighty degree turn, I now felt as though I had something to aspire to. Not a *suit*, working the nine to five gruel with a mountain of debts. Not someone, who beneath the smiles and the handshakes, hides a life so full of stress and worry, most of which are caused by things that don't even exist or truly matter. Not a guy who has a two-week break each year to escape his woes and long weekends spent trying to escape the rat race, only to join his breed in the pubs and clubs still bound by the dress codes and rules of false smiles that bind him the other five days each week. The guidance counsellors back at school had obviously forgotten to tell us that life wasn't limited to work and study, there was a third factor that Noodle had found and its name was *play*.

The joints continued to come our way and we somehow got a beer from a latecomer who'd squeezed himself between Ben and I, causing us to socialise with strangers for the first time that evening.

Feeling nature's call, I got up and headed for the nearby rocks. Walking back, I watched as more wood was being thrown onto the dwindling blaze, causing sparks to jump out around the fire. As I glanced over at Noodle and his girl he beckoned me over with a wave of his hand but paranoid, in case it wasn't me that he was signalling to, I approached with hesitation. Luckily his smile grew as I approached. Sitting down next to him, a wave of bonfire smoke hit my face blinding me as sparks from the fire jumped towards us.

'How are you doing Matt?' Noodle coughed out, trying hard to hold eye contact through the smog that was blowing our way from the fire. Through my own watering eyes I watched as his head nodded to the rhythm of the music.

'Cool,' I said trying my hardest to be exactly that and as quickly as it had come, the wind swung back and the smoke cleared.

Noodle started telling me about his travels, pleased to have a keen listener. His beautiful girlfriend turned out to be an Australian called Fran, who was in her second month of a work visa in England.

They'd met in the French Alps when he'd gone for a short snowboarding trip earlier in the year, having spent the bulk of the winter travelling around Indonesia and Australia. From his stories it seemed his favourite place to travel in was Indonesia. It was somewhere I'd heard of but couldn't have placed on a world map. Noodle explained that it was in Asia, which helped me somewhat but its exact whereabouts didn't matter. Noodle claimed you could easily live on three pounds a day in some parts, covering accommodation, food and beer. Best of all, he enthusiastically explained, the surf was world class. My knowledge of the world was as weak as my own travel experience, which stretched as far as family holidays to Wales and a day in Scotland. However, it seemed to me that if such places were real the whole world would want to live there. As far as I could see, either the rest of the world did not know this lifestyle existed or else Noodle was just talking drunken bollocks. It sounded like fantasy, but Fran backed up Noodle's facts, making me believe without further question.

Passing another joint across to me, Fran told me of her own experience in Asia. She had travelled around India and Nepal, and like Noodle's experience in Indonesia, had found it both cheap and beautiful, yet sadly poverty stricken. Unlike Noodle, she'd gone there for the culture rather than just the cheap prices and good surf.

'Everybody gets something different out of travelling. I left Oz to see some culture in Asia and Europe, while Noodle's trips are motivated only by surfing. Not that there's anything wrong with that. If you want to travel, you need to think about what you want to get out of the experience and let that determine where you go,' words of advice that sounded better than anything I'd heard in school, but Noodle clinched the idea of travelling for me when he said 'Or if you want beautiful chicks lying around in bikinis all day, go to Oz,' receiving a playful punch from Fran.

As Noodle began to go into more depth about Australia, I knew I had to go there. The more he told me, the better it sounded, particularly a small east coast town called Byron Bay, that according to Noodle, was run by hippies and surfers and oozed a laid back atmosphere, sun, women and of course, good surf. All, including the surf, were becoming the essential ingredients in creating a map of my future travel plans.

I don't know if it was the weed or the environment but it all sounded so good, I could go to Asia for cheap prices and some culture, and Australia for surf. Only a few things were stopping me buying a ticket and being seventeen with no money, no passport and a year of school left to complete, was a sizeable roadblock in my path that wasn't likely to shift for a while yet.

Across the fire I could see Ben having a laugh with two girls, the closest to him had bleached blonde dreadlocks and she looked a little wasted. The other girl looked closer to our age and undoubtedly his best chance of pulling. If experience had taught me anything, then it was that when you're seventeen, pulling another seventeen year old is hard but to get with an older girl is about as easy as dragging a bus full of pensioners up a hill with your teeth. Looking back over, I decided to leave the hard work to Ben for the weekend, I was too absorbed with the thought of travel to give thought to anything else.

I don't remember being the last one at the fire but the next thing I knew, I had woken up alone on the beach in an eerie morning light. The tide had dropped right out and the fire had long died. The time escaped me but the sun was still hidden behind the horizon. As I sat up rubbing my eyes and brushing off the sand that had stuck to my face and clothes, I tried to take stock of my environment. Further down the beach I could see a surfer in a wetsuit entering the glassy looking water. The wind was calm and the waves looked so alluring that I felt like joining the lone surfer for a swim but I was held back by the suspicion that the water wasn't going be particularly warm without a wetsuit.

Walking back across the sand, I watched the sun rise over the town. It all seemed so peaceful, the only sign of life were surfers pulling up in their cars and struggling to fit into their skin-tight wetsuits, a far cry from how the beach would be in a few hours. The conversations with Noodle and Fran began to come back to me, their choice of lifestyle just as desirable as it had appeared the night before. The idea of backpacking was feeling a lot more achievable now than it ever had before.

Climbing up onto the top bunk, I noticed that Ben was snoring but more importantly, he was alone, as I knew it would have been sheer hell if he'd somehow pulled and I'd not. When I woke up again I realised that my clothes, which I was still wearing, reeked of smoke from the fire. The room was empty again for the second day running, which made me think that I must either snore very loudly or smell even worse than I already knew I did.

Making my way downstairs, I realised that all we had left were a couple of hours until the weekend was over and a train would take us back to our hometown of ugly office buildings and warehouses. The people around us would change from happy, free and tanned to tense, trapped and pale. It was a different world but not so far away, same language, same currency, just different choices and priorities.

Choosing to walk to the train station through the town we spotted Noodle and a couple of other guys speeding our way on skateboards. The three of them were weaving all over the road and pavement, setting themselves up for various obstacles around which to perform flawless tricks. As they drew closer Noodle looked our way and shouted 'Oi Oi!' and gave us a wave, before speeding away in the opposite direction.

From the train, the countryside changed to town and back again. Everywhere we stopped was now intriguing me. I wanted to get off and explore, do anything but go home to the same old place again. For one reason or another I'd never been outside of Britain, never flown and probably because of that, it was all I could think of wanting to do. In comparison, Ben had been abroad nearly every year of his life although usually to visit family in the States, something that always made me envious, the furthest away my relations lived was London.

Discussions changed as the days flew by. Our friends soon tired of our stories and ideas to travel. School began again in September and the words *university and career* became a regular topic amongst us all, although Ben and I made plans to go backpacking together just as soon as school was over and we'd saved a little spending money working through the following summer. Asia and Australia were set to be our destinations, but we still had a year of school ahead to work on the finer details so we put the plans on a back burner and focussed on getting through school.

Two
10 months later…

There was a recurring dream that plagued me throughout my last year at school. It was about a large, dark brown horse with a white streak down his nose. Whether or not I was actually the horse in the dreams I could never tell, although I could certainly see his dilemma. He was stuck in a tiny paddock, so small that, try as he might, the horse could never break into a full gallop, which was all he ever wanted to do. So day in, day out, the horse would trot around looking for the best run up but it would always be in vain and he'd end up snorting and kicking out in sheer frustration.

I never saw the horse make it. Just as he got ever so close I'd always wake up, to an annoying alarm beep. Pressing the snooze button for another five minutes, I would will the dream back to see the horse galloping but by then the paddock had vanished, scared off by the flashing numbers and shrill sounds of technology.

My real world, for my entire life of eighteen years and twenty-nine days, was at that point, one of concrete and traffic. I was born into an M4 corridor town, less than an hour away from the giant concrete mass affectionately known as London, within half an hour drive away from five similar dirty, overdeveloped, doppelganger towns, and hours away from the nearest beach. Over the years that I'd spent living in the same house on the same road, I had watched as ugly office buildings sprang up like weeds, knowing that eventually one of them would become my life, stripping away the sunniest days of the summers and the fresh chill of winter. The seasons, like the years, would be viewed through tinted windows and only experienced at weekends.

Perhaps after a few years it wouldn't seem so bad. The problem was I really didn't want to find out. School was slamming the brakes on and coming to the end of the road, which meant decisions had to be made for a trip that should have been well past the planning stage by now. At least in the past few months I'd experienced a late growing spurt, shooting up a few inches and beginning to look my age, although there was still no sign of any stubble. So, looking older, I began to feel a little older and more equipped for all that the world had to throw at me.

15

Hitting the snooze button on my alarm for the third time, I knew it would have to be my last. Beyond the closed curtains, I could predict the weather outside. Light shone through but not like the bright rays that instantly bring warmth to the room. No, this was a muffled glow meaning only one thing; once again the sun was hidden by depressing, summertime drizzle.

Within seconds under the shower, my wet brown hair was plastered to my forehead by the cool spray but it did little to wake me up. It was nearly July and still we had to suffer the grey skies and rain that were meant to plague only the winters. However, now it was too mild for a jacket but too windy for an umbrella so I knew I'd be getting wet. A second chance, I thought, to wake up properly.

Styling my short hair, I put on my shirt, trousers and tie, a sixth form uniform that was designed to adapt me for a life of office work, regardless of the future I would choose. It was the last time I'd have to follow this routine though, as my final three hour A-Level exam was just over an hour away and I had no intention of winding up sat in a stuffy office dressed like a sixth former.

Opening the front door I paused to think about the significance this damp, summer morning was about to play in my life. Thirteen years of studying, homework, coursework, exams, classes, teachers and headmasters were finally over, or at least they would be in about four and a half hours, when I would step back out into the wet afternoon air and away from the examination hall.

Stopping momentarily to check that I'd packed a pen, I quickly unzipped my worn out rucksack, which had become personalised over the past year with *mellow*, a word I'd borrowed from Noodle's sweater the night of the beach party, written across the top in bold white Tipp-Ex lettering. Finding one well chewed blue biro, I headed out, slamming the front door to alert the world of my departure.

The exam I was slowly trudging towards was for film studies and so my revision had consisted of studying films. Not the revolutionary Soviet films of the 1930s that made up the curriculum and which bored me in class, but rather the surfing variety. I watched in awe as daredevil surfers took off on thirty-foot waves, only to slip off half way along and get pounded into the raw energy of the fierce looking surf. I'd seen *Big Wednesday,* a surfing classic, for the hundredth time and always marvelled at the carefree lifestyles of the protagonists that were depicted through the camera lens. I didn't watch them instead of the Soviet flicks because I was feeling cocky about the exam and certainly not because I planned to write a two thousand word essay about them. No, I spent my precious last few hours pausing frames and rewinding scenes because I had wanted to go into the exam knowing exactly why it had to be my last.

Achieving good grades in exams had never been a top priority on my list of life ambitions. Wedged somewhere between getting a career and a mortgage, it lay snugly at the bottom of the heap. 'Grades and exams all mean shit at the end of the day anyway, unless you're headed for university,' my sister Rachel had told me back when I was at the eager age of fifteen, a year before sitting my GCSE exams. She boasted that she had managed to get a well-paid job without having achieved decent grades and so her mentality was that it was all a waste of time trying. 'They're only interested in knowing that you didn't drop out at sixteen or that you're not a dunce. Although there are exceptions,' she told me, as I listened wide-eyed, studying from the nineteen-year-old master. 'If you want to be a doctor or an astronaut you'll need the grades but I can't see you doing either of those.'
'No way,' I concurred.
'And likewise if you want to go to university you'll need certain grades, although you can normally scrape by without everything they ask for. That said, some of my friends who are at uni complain about being skint and all the studying they're expected to do, neither of which really compare to earning a wage in the real world and having money to spend.'
'Neither sound that great really,' I added, knocking her off her stride.
'Look Mattie, all I'm saying is that you can still get a good job without amazing grades, so don't get too stressed out with revision and things, okay?'
'Okay,' I agreed. Feeling confident that what she was telling me was gospel.

Call it a blessing or a curse, I'd developed a knack of being able to pass through my early schooling comfortably, all the while putting in the least possible effort. In school, the teachers had always criticised me for it, always ready to inform my parents that with a little hard work I could be capable of so much more. The problem was, I was getting good enough results so there was nothing motivating me to try harder. Sixth form was different though, I found subjects that I was genuinely interested in and so I exerted more time and effort, not for the grades but because the notion of spending two years studying

17

subjects such as film and social studies seemed like an interesting thing to do, before moving towards the life I longed for.

Climbing up the steep hill that led to the school entrance, I turned off my ipod and straightened my damp hair in the reflection of a car window.

'I was thinking you'd overslept,' a familiar voice called from behind. Pulling a pair of silent headphones out from my ears, I spun around to see Kermit. A lanky six-foot-two schoolmate, with a four-inch afro sprouting out like a fuzzy mushroom on top of his long face. His name had derived from a much publicised virginity loss to a girl that bore a frighteningly close resemblance to Miss Piggy.

'Kermit! Hey mate, I must say that I was tempted to stay in bed, especially given the weather. How are you feeling?' I asked, knowing he was prone to big nerves prior to exams.

'I'll be better this afternoon after a few pints. Yourself?'

'I'm feeling ready, in fact I've been ready for this day to come for years,' I declared.

'Well at least for you it's all over Matt. If I don't perform I don't get into uni,' Kermit stressed.

'I'm sure you'll be fine, but we'd better go,' I said, beginning to walk before spotting Ben at the bottom of the hill.

'Shit Ben, you look exhausted,' Kermit exclaimed as Ben came closer. 'Don't tell me you were up studying all night?'

'No, I wasn't studying, I just couldn't sleep so I watched that Nicole Kidman movie on Sky until about three,' he replied, stroking his goatee. A habit I recognised as a sign he was lying. Not even Kermit spent as many hours studying as Ben was known to do. Like myself, Ben had a notoriously short attention span in class but whereas the information somehow sank into my brain, for him it seemed to pass on through one of his ears and out the other without any interference. Like Kermit, he was also planning to go to university but not until he'd enjoyed a year backpacking around the world with me.

Taking our places in the spacious exam room I found myself sitting next to Ben, separated by an even metre. It was the worst place to seat a friend, any mutual glances could be considered cheating and there would always be the risk of laughter erupting over nothing. Kermit, on the other hand, was sitting his maths exam in another hall, probably too nervous to look anywhere but at the paper.

The exam seemed pretty easy, although the time certainly dragged towards the end. As I stared blankly at the stout examiner a few metres away, she appeared to be equally bored, although I doubted that she too harboured the thoughts of breaking the silence with a hum or willed someone's phone to go off.

Pushing my plastic chair neatly beneath the small wooden table, it hadn't registered in my mind, but I was finally free. Outside in the drizzle, I was shaking hands with my fellow classmates and dishing out a good measure of congratulations but still it didn't click. Twenty minutes later sat inside a fast food outlet and tucking into a greasy double cheeseburger, the fact that we were finished finally registered in my mind.

'*Guys*, do you realise we're all *free*? For the first time in our lives, we're adults with no more school, no jobs and certainly no … children,' as the last word left my lips, I watched as a familiar face struggled to get her pram and a young boy through the restaurant doors. No one else took any notice of her but then nobody else got their first ever snog from her, aged eleven. She'd been in my tutor group throughout school, or at least the first three years, when she'd disappeared from school to have her first child. Obviously the family had grown since then, a scary thought but not such a big surprise. We'd all noticed that having a baby was something of a status symbol for some teenage girls in our town, either that or there was an incredible amount of defective contraception knocking around. What the babies' fathers think about it is anybody's guess; you never see them. Passing my table, we paid no heed to each other, although I couldn't help but feel glad our relationship had ended after a couple of snogs. Otherwise, I might have been another doomed teenage father, oddly absent from the picture.

'Sixth form has definitely been fun though,' Kermit stated.
'Better than normal school had been, yeah! But university's where the real fun's at,' replied Ben. He'd always talked of going to university, along with Kermit but lately such topics had begun to take precedence over my favourite subject.
'University!' I grimaced, 'you chumps can spend another few years of study and exams, qualifying for some job or other that you'll never even end up doing. Meanwhile I'll be kicking back on a tropical island somewhere, with a sun kissed honey on each arm. Besides which Ben, I guarantee that by the time we come back from our trip, you'll be as hooked on travel as I think I already am and university will be right out the window.'

'Oh, here we go, the old travel bug huh Matt?' Kermit piped up, in a bored voice. 'A fiver says that by the time both Ben and I have degrees and top jobs, you'll be working here in this shit hole, doing that guy's job,' he said, pointing towards a spotty burger flipper handing out change to my one time girlfriend.

'Are you both honestly telling me that, on the blazing hot days of summer, you'd rather be sitting in an air-conditioned building, than on a beach?' I asked, knowing I was fighting a well-trodden losing battle.

'No, not at all but I'll be taking tropical holidays every year once I've got a good job and money,' Kermit replied. 'Besides, you won't be able to live that life forever, at some point every backpacker has to stop travelling and grow up.'

'Perhaps, but it's a dream worth chasing.'

Stepping back out into the rain, we decided to head for our local pub, The Flying Duck. A building with a dozen small rooms branching off one another and low ceilings with wooden beams that jumped out and struck the odd careless drunk. Regular as clockwork every Friday and Saturday night we'd be sat in the corner of the same room. The experience of trying another pub would have been welcomed as far as I was concerned, but breaking habit was considered a taboo among the group, who'd become settled with the routine and felt happy in the familiar surroundings.

Sitting down at our table and sending out a few text messages to the rest of our group, the beers went down a treat. As our afternoon talks moved back and forth between the impending future and the distant past, we all had an embarrassing tale to tell about another at the table as we had all shared the same good times over the past few years. It was a great feeling to be a part of something so special and at the same time I found it strange to think it was all coming to an end.

Watching Ben get up for a cigarette, I decided to follow him out and get an update on our travel plans. Walking out of the front door, a familiar face from the past was coming in the other way. Frozen to the spot, I watched as Lola breezed past, oblivious of my presence.

Turning back around and following her to the bar, she glanced up in my direction, no doubt feeling followed. As soon as she saw me, a friendly and extremely memorable smile flashed across her face, breaking down the barriers of time since we'd last met.

Even though I already had an older sister, as a child I'd claimed Lola to be an honorary adopted sibling. In fact, I'd always gotten on much better with her than I did my own sister, once trying to convince my parents to swap them. She was Rachel's best friend and the pair of them were inseparable, as were our mums, right up until tragedy struck. Her dad had left for work one morning but a tired lorry driver on the motorway stopped him from ever making it. In what seemed like days later, although I'm sure it was more like months, her Mum decided to move back to her childhood village in Cornwall, taking Lola away from us. After that our families drifted a little, Rachel and Lola's letters to each other began to dry up and eventually she vanished from our lives.

'Lola? What on earth are you doing here?' I smiled as she clocked me looking in disbelief at the woman before me. Her smile was as I remembered but this was a beautiful grown woman standing before me; worn out trainers, baggy faded jeans and a red vest top. Her long brown hair was matted into dreadlocks and tied back, and a small silver hoop protruded from her plucked eyebrows.

'Little Mattie? Oh my God! Look at you, all grown up. How long has it been eight? ... Ten years?' her arms opened wide, for a hug and a sisterly kiss on the cheek. Pulling away, lost in a comfortable silence, I had a thousand questions to ask but only one reached my lips.

'Do you want a drink?' I muttered.

'Okay yeah, Jack and coke, thanks Mattie,' she responded, staring at me, seemingly as bewildered by our meeting as I was.

'So... What the hell are you doing here?' I asked as we waited for the drinks.

'I'm just passing through, staying with Sadie for the night before flying off to Thailand tomorrow afternoon,' she said. In my mind I pictured Sadie, a large girl with a friendly face, another of Rachel's old friends whom I hadn't seen for some years.

'I tried to call your sister, I wanted to have a little reunion, get the girls together again, you know? But I couldn't get hold of her and Andrea couldn't get a babysitter. So it's just the two of us. Cheers!' Lola said, taking her drink and clinking it against my pint.

'Did you say you're going to Thailand?'

'Tomorrow,' she answered with a smug grin.

'Wow. How long for?' I asked, always fascinated to hear about someone's travels.

'Well, I want to spend two months in South-East Asia, travelling around Thailand, Laos, Vietnam and Cambodia. Probably, only a couple of those weeks will be spent in Thailand, hopefully to do a little diving.'

'Cool. Sounds great, I'm going to Thailand myself soon,' I announced.

'Oh yeah, when?' her eyes lit up, before adding, 'shall we sit down?' before I could respond.

Deciding to find a different table to our friends, Lola and I cut through to another quieter room where I began to go into the details of the trip Ben and I were soon to embark upon. We did a quick calculation and realised we'd probably miss each other in Thailand by six weeks. Lola revealed that she too was destined for Australia after Asia but that was to be a quick pit stop before a planned six or so months in New Zealand. The more we talked the more I was fascinated to learn about Lola's recent past. She was now twenty-two and had ventured out to Ghana on a work placement, straight after university, before going down to South Africa for two months of backpacking.

'I guess the travel bug took a stronger hold on me than I'd ever imagined it could,' she smiled. 'When I set out for Ghana, I had every intention of settling down in Plymouth and even after my six months there were up I still felt that's what I wanted. But sitting on the plane home from Cape Town, I reflected on my trip and I started to cry at the thought of leaving it all behind. It was then that it dawned on me, just what I was giving up and going back to. I mean, I don't want to travel forever but I've definitely got another trip or two in me before I want to settle down,' she added.

'So are you travelling alone?' I asked.

'Yeah, but that's okay. You're only as lonely as you want to be. With so many other backpackers in the same boat, I'll make plenty of friends along the way.'

'Right,' I commented, a little sceptically, glad that I wasn't having to test that theory. 'So where's Sadie?'

'She's working. I couldn't get a later train up, so I thought I'd kill a couple of hours here. It's good to see you again though Mattie. How's Rachel getting on?'

The afternoon drifted by as Lola and I talked about Rachel and caught up on a decade of missed stories and adventures. Ben had come looking for me but after reintroducing the pair, who had only met a handful of times as children, he skulked off back to his table. When the time came for her to leave and head to Sadie's house I wanted to go with her, not just to Sadie's but to Thailand.

'Here's my email, let me know when you're in Thailand, just in case things change and I'm still there,' she said, passing a small piece of paper across the table as she stood up.

'Let's hope so,' I said, giving her another hug and watching her go, before I made my way back to my friends.

Taking my seat next to Kermit, I felt like September couldn't come quickly enough, I wanted to be the one flying away tomorrow. As I tried to make conversation with Ben about our plans, possibly even bringing them forwards, he seemed aloof and the hours of drinking were beginning to take a hold of him, so I decided to wait for a better time.

August eighteenth, results day, arrived with an assortment of trepidation and relief for us all. Whatever the day had in store for me was fine, I knew it wouldn't bring about any huge revelations or immediate changes. Others would see their futures become a firm step closer or fly away like a plastic bag in the wind, hinging on just how they'd performed during the most important few hours of their entire schooling. The pressure and significance of the day lingered among us like a dirty thought in a clean mind. Some of my friends were even in store for money and materialistic rewards, if their demanding parents felt they'd lived up to expectations. My dad would no doubt direct me to a cold can of beer in the fridge, whilst my mum would smile and try in vain to persuade me to go to university. That was my reward and that would be all I needed or wanted.

The sky was overcast and grey for the first time in over a week, turning the air thick and humid, and bringing back memories from our exam time. The past two months of sunshine since the exams had been spent working full time in a windowless warehouse, packing boxes. Paradoxically, it was exactly what I was working to get away from and hardly the most stimulating choice of work but I had sworn to avoid offices by any means. Although I knew that summer was just beyond the walls, I focused on saving every penny for the trip and couldn't help but see the irony of the rain on one of my rare days off.

'So have you booked the flight yet you two?' Kermit asked Ben and I, as we climbed the hill to school for one last time. It had been a couple of weeks since I'd seen Kermit. I was stuck in a warehouse and he'd landed a job in a neighbouring town, the both of us becoming rare sights.

'In a few days,' Ben responded, giving Kermit the same line I'd been hearing for the past few weeks.

'What's taking you so long? You've got the money for the ticket now, right?'

'The problem is more agreeing on our itinerary than our shortcomings on the financial side. But we're definitely going to sort it out this week, *right* Ben?' I asked, my doubt at his commitment becoming hard to hide.

'Yeah, course. I can't wait to head out and shag some Aussie girls,' he said with an exaggerated confidence.

Inside, the building was even stuffier than the humid air outside. Familiar faces, classmates and teachers, from the past few years of my life, were all around the big hall, nervously chatting, celebrating and in a couple of cases, crying.

Results envelopes in hand, Kermit opened his first, silently reading his paper. His face was stone cold not showing any emotion. Putting the paper back into the envelope he let out a tiny smile, which then grew uncontrollably bigger.

'All good,' he announced, with a huge grin, 'A in Psychology, B's in Maths and Biology. Looks like I'm going to Sheffield then lads,' we both took turns in shaking his hand and giving him praise. It was better than he'd been expecting but then he'd certainly worked hard for it.

I went next, momentarily building up the suspense as I silently read the results.

'Not bad,' I said folding the paper up and stuffing it into my pocket.

'What do you mean not bad? What the hell did you get then?' Ben asked, after I ushered for him to go on and read his own.

'Straight B's,' I quietly whispered, as though I was worried about anyone overhearing.

'No way... There's got to be a mix-up, you slept through most of your classes,' Ben protested.

'*You jammy git*,' Kermit added, laughing and extending his hand in congratulations. In a way I felt like a cheat, as I knew Ben and Kermit had truly worked for theirs, while I had breezed through doing the least work possible.

Finally it was Ben's turn. Ripping the envelope open, he glanced at the contents and scrunched his face up, muttering '*Fuck,*' before turning and walking away from us towards the door, pulling a packet of cigarettes out of his pocket as he went. Watching him go, Kermit and I glanced at each other in shock, before quickly following.

Outside, Ben was sat on a metal bench as he had been so many times before over the years. This time smoking a cigarette and looking as though his world had just caved in.

'Two C's and a D,' he shouted, as we got closer. 'May as well be three fucking F's... so much for deferring a year.'

'I reckon you need a pint or two mate,' Kermit said after a moment of silence, as Ben picked himself up from the bench and followed us away from the school.

'So what are your plans now?' Kermit asked Ben when we'd all got pints and sat down at our usual spot in the pub.

'He's going to screw what the examination board had to say and come travelling for a year before becoming a lifetime member of the backpacking lifestyle,' I answered on his behalf.

'No, I think that's your plan Matt. I might have to stay here and resit my exams,' Ben solemnly said, as I waited for the punch line.

'You're not serious, surely?' I asked. Seeing my own plans now crumbling away.

'What other options do I have? I need to go to university, I can't just breeze through life like you Matt.'

'What do you mean *breeze through*?' I interrupted, feeling a little offended and sitting up to take in exactly what he was saying. 'Are you honestly telling me that you're considering staying here and going back to school?'

'I'm not considering it, I'm saying that I am *going to do it*. Backpacking is something that I can do after university. Australia will still be there, Thailand will still be there, they'll just have to wait, that's all.'

I couldn't believe my ears, it sounded as though he was backing out of our trip, although the Ben I knew wouldn't do that, not to a mate, not a month before we were due to go. As he continued to ramble on and explain himself further, I wasn't interested in listening and so got up for a walk outside. My head was beginning to fill with visions of growing old in the warehouse, still packing boxes, ranting to strangers of the time that I nearly travelled, nearly escaped, like Uncle Albert's war stories.

Following me out, Ben called from behind me, 'I'm really sorry mate. If I had got the grades I needed then you know I would have deferred and come along. If I go now though then it'll be even harder to resit later, especially after a year of fun in the sun. You're still going to go though, right?' he asked, before lighting up. Throwing him a look of false hurt, my cocky smile rose to the surface. 'Of course,' I replied, 'just means all the more foreign honey for me,' I said, although doubtful if I could really travel alone.

Back inside the pub, I calmed down and began to look at the situation as a positive. Ben was suffering more than me and it was unfair to assume that he would put his university hopes aside for a few months of fun. So, as the drinks continued to flow throughout the rest of the day and into the evening, I began plotting my solo route, even feeling a little more freedom by the notion that I no longer had to wait for Ben to get his act together.

'Christ Matthew, you look like death. I assume you were partying after your results,' my mother said without the slightest hint of sympathy in her voice as I entered the kitchen, the following morning.

'Errrrrrmmm, what time is it?' I slurred, realising I was still dressed in my shorts and surf t-shirt which I'd worn the previous day.

'It's twelve-twenty, are you going to tell me what you got then?' she asked.

'Oh, oh yeah. Twelve-twenty?' I repeated, fumbling in my pocket for the result paper, just in case I got it wrong from my hazy memory, 'here,' I said, pushing the crumpled envelope into her hands as I headed for the kettle.

'Wow, Matt these are great. Are you pleased?' she said, holding the piece of paper up.

'Yeah, I guess. Where are the tea bags?'

'All gone I'm afraid. You'll have to have a coffee and you can make me one while you're at it.'

'So does this mean you'll reconsider university?' she asked.

'No, but Ben is,' I groaned.

'I thought Ben was always going, right after your travels?' she asked.

'Well, yes and no. He didn't quite get the grades he wanted, so he's got to retake them.'

'Oh no,' my mother replied, 'so he won't be travelling?' she asked.

'Nope,' I bluntly responded, frustrations at his decision rising again.

'So what are *you* going to do?' she asked, taking the mug of coffee.

'I'm still going.'

'What backpacking? *Alone*?' her voice beginning to tremble, 'Matthew you're *only* eighteen, you *are not* going half way across the world *alone*. It's a crazy world out there, I've got to admit I wasn't keen on you going with Ben but I got used to it, *but this*, no, *no way*.'

'What do you mean *no*? Mum I'm not asking you if I can do this, I'm telling you this is what I'm going to do. People do it all the time, at my age and younger. Even Lola's travelling alone,' I couldn't believe I was having this conversation; it was like being seventeen again and asking to go to Newquay for a weekend.

'Believe me, Sandra's not happy about her little girl travelling alone either. Look, maybe in a year or two when you're older and more responsible. You've got the grades for university, why don't you go and then you and Ben can both travel together afterwards?'

'No way. I'm eighteen mum, not a kid. I'm going, that's all there is to it,' I declared, picking up my coffee and making a hasty retreat to my bedroom.

'Well, you're certainly acting like a grown up! I hope you called in at work this morning,' she nagged, as I walked away.

'Called in?'

'Well you're obviously not there, so I assume you phoned them to let them know.'

'Shiiittttt,' I groaned and headed upstairs to find my phone.

September soon came around but it didn't mean the beginning of my trip. Sipping at my pint of Fosters, I watched as Ben approached our corner of the pub. It had been a few weeks since I'd seen or spoken to him, deciding instead to bury myself in my work and travel plans.

'Still here? I thought you were going to Thailand this month Matt,' Ben teased me, oblivious to my frustration that I was still around.

'Slight delay on that but the flight's booked for the third of December,' I replied with ice in my voice.

'Oh wow,' Ben said, 'you didn't tell me you'd booked the flight. But why December, I thought our plan was for September?'

'*Our plan* was, but early December's a lot cheaper, flight wise,' I said, biting my tongue after learning from the travel agent that if I'd booked the flight months earlier, when Ben was dithering, then I'd have been able to get a better deal for September.

'Well, at least you can save a little more money then,' he smiled. Although the thought of two more months of work in the warehouse had worn mine thin.

I left the pub early that night and walked home through the chilly northerly wind. The urge to go travelling was getting stronger

27

and stronger all the time. At home I was still getting grief from my mum, who'd been visibly shocked when I announced my confirmed flight date, hurt at my choice to leave before Christmas, although my plan had always been that way.

Finally, after what seemed like an eternity of hoping, planning and dreaming, the final weeks ticked away until all that was left was a last night at The Flying Duck. The majority of my friends were there, including Kermit who'd taken a brief break from university to say goodbye.

Surprisingly, there were still doubts among them that I would last the intended year and a few expectations that I'd bottle out at the airport. However, none of these doubts came from Ben as he, more than anyone, knew just how determined I was to leave and make a go of my dreams. An unfamiliar girl was sat at Ben's side, a redhead called Tara, who sat in silence for the first half hour, laughing quietly at Ben's jokes before finally opening her mouth and speaking.

'You're so lucky to be going. Ben talks about you all the time, about how jealous he is and how he has plans to do the same as soon he's finished university,' she said.

'Ben'll go, I'm sure,' I said, hoping I was right.

'You know Matt, you shouldn't count me out. Who knows, maybe I'll get sick of college and join you for a few months,' Ben said but it was a hollow remark and behind his words I could see there was no real intent.

'Well, we all chipped in and got you a little present,' Kermit said, interrupting us as he returned from the bar.

'Not that you'll have much use for it though,' Ben added. This was followed by a collective knowing laughter around the table. Stripping the paper off, I got the joke, sadly though it seemed *I was it*.

'Condoms, *ribbed no less*. Thanks everyone, you shouldn't have, or at least you could have got me more than just three, they'll be used up on the plane. What about the year that follows?'

'Matt, I know you haven't flown before but you should know that airlines don't take kindly to passengers blowing up condoms on the flight,' Kermit joked.

'I guarantee you'll still have them, with the box unopened, by the time you fly back next December. In fact, I will bet you that during the next year… no, the next month that you can't find three different willing and able ladies, to help you use them up,' Ben said, 'and by ladies I don't mean *lady boys*, okay?' he joked.

'Three girls? In one month? He'll never manage it. Let's make it a year,' Kermit remarked.

'Ho, ho. Come on, look, I'll take the bet of one month, let you know what you're missing out on. In fact, let's say from tomorrow until New Year's Day, so just under a month,' I said, with offhanded confidence.

'You wish. You've slept with how many, thus far? Two?' Ben announced to the world, making my cheeks blush, before he laid down the glove. 'What do you say Matt, do you accept the challenge placed before you? Three different women from tomorrow the third of December, when you fly to Thailand, until the morning of New Year's Day, in Australia. None can have been paid for and we need photographic proof of at least two of them, the other I can accept as probably having vanished after what would no doubt be the biggest mistake of the poor girl's life,' Ben joked

'And what exactly is at stake?' I asked, bemused by his challenge.

'Legendary status, what else? Gathered around this table are the majority of the people you call friends in this town. So, just as Kermit will always have that unfortunate name for shagging Miss Piggy, you'll always be remembered as the guy who went travelling round the world and pulled for his country. *Matt, the master of foreign poontang*, simple as that.'

'Fair enough,' I said smiling at the thought of succeeding, 'I accept that challenge, although it's hardly going to be difficult,' I swaggered, before knocking back my drink and pocketing the condoms.

'Baby brother!' Rachel yelled out, busting into my room and switching the light on and off like a strobe. 'Why is it we've all got up at this ungodly hour to take you to the airport and you're still in bed? You're not having second thoughts about going are you?' she joked as I tried to prise my sleepy eyes open. Leaving the light on as she retreated I checked for signs of a hangover before looking at the time. Good news and bad news, my head was clear but I had ten minutes until my ideal departure time.

Dashing in and out of the shower, I threw on my clothes, quickly styled my hair, grabbed my wallet and phone and dashed downstairs, where my new backpack and *mellow* bag, that would serve as my hand luggage, were both waiting. I felt like a young Indiana Jones, about to head out on my first ever adventure and like his quick hat grab in the face of imminent danger, I realised I'd left the condoms in my other jeans, which were being left behind, and made a scramble back up the stairs, dodging Rachel and my dad who were headed in the opposite direction. Quickly transferring them over into my pocket, I dashed back down to find the front door open waiting for me to escape through.

Driving up the ramp in the airport car park, I felt in absolute awe of my surroundings. I'd always lived near the Heathrow flight paths, yet this was my first time at the airport. On any blue-sky day, I could look up at any given time of day and I was guaranteed to see at least two planes soaring above. I'd spent my whole life watching these pass on by, wishing I was one of the lucky passengers looking down upon the tiny world below and smiling knowing they were headed for somewhere different, not necessarily better but different. Those people were the envy of my childhood and finally I was joining their ranks, *I* was going to look out on the tiny world below and smile.

Queuing up for the baggage check-in, dad tried to talk me through the procedure, having flown with work a couple of times. However I was too preoccupied with a beautiful young woman with a blonde ponytail poking out through the hole in her baseball cap. She was sitting down, just a few people ahead of me in the immobile queue, using her backpack as a seat. I instantly sized her up as five-foot-eight and twenty-one, maybe twenty-two-years-old. She too appeared to be travelling alone.

'How good would it be to sit next to *her* for the eleven hour flight?' I quietly asked my dad, although he didn't hear me, his attention on one of the pretty airline staff seated behind the counter.

I watched studiously as the blonde approached a desk and handed her backpack over, wondering if I could request a seat beside her. But as it came to my turn to check in, all I could do was ask for a window seat, as I handed my bag over.

Walking back to my farewell party my mum suggested we go for breakfast, but I wasn't interested. I just wanted to board the plane and get to Thailand. So, passport in hand, I made my way over to the departure gate, the final stop before heading on through, beyond no-man's-land. Giving my tearful mum a hug goodbye, I repeated the process with my less emotional dad and sister, before turning to walk away. With every step, emotions flooded my mind, anxiety, excitement and nervousness. I was finally on my way.

Three

Walking into the departure lounge at Heathrow was disappointing. In my mind I'd conjured up an image that was full of intrepid explorer types and people dashing for their planes, but rather it was more like a shopping centre, and I immediately began to regret not having breakfast with my family. As I'd queued for the metal detector there had been an brief urge to turn back around and abandon my dream, secretly head to Wales and become a shepherd, all the while sending fabricated postcards from rare and unusual locations. Fortunately, as I stepped ever closer I began to picture the places I would actually be sending postcards from.

Taking a seat underneath a couple of monitors updating flight information, I had just over two hours to kill but no money to spend. Well not in the designer airport shops anyhow. Putting on my iPod, my mind was fluctuating between highs and lows, as I began to think a little too much about everything that lay ahead of me. Every minute spent in the departure lounge seemed like torture, I just wanted to get on the plane. So I was devastated when, after finally calling my flight, I found myself in another waiting area and worst of all, as much as I looked around, I couldn't see the blonde.

At last, the moment came and I stepped onto my first aeroplane, feeling like a five year old in awe of my surroundings. I was amazed at the sheer size of the thing. To get to my seat I had to walk past at least a couple of hundred other seats and there were still more on the other side. The awe didn't stop there, as I proceeded to fiddle with everything my seat had to offer, like a child in a toyshop.

I had a window seat, which was what I'd asked for, but beyond the windows the sky was still dark which limited my chances to see my old town from the *other* perspective. The two seats that separated me from the aisle were vacant, opening up the possibility that if nobody sat down then I could stretch across. Those hopes, along with those that the blonde would be sat next to me, were dashed when a trim couple in their mid-fifties stopped beside me, placing their bags in the overhead rack before squeezing into the two vacant seats.

They hadn't been seated for more than a minute before the lady sat next me turned and sized me up, opening her mouth, 'Are you particularly fond of window seats?' she asked with a motherly tone. A little unsure just how to answer, I hesitated for a moment, thinking that of the things I was fond of, window seats wouldn't have ranked very highly. 'Er, no,' I replied.

'Oh well, in that case, could I trouble you to swap? I get awfully nervous flying and find looking out the window really helps,' she said.

'Yeah, sure,' I answered, thinking that I didn't really want to be trapped next to a nervous flyer. So we all got back up and the couple went in first, leaving me on the aisle. With a quiet 'thank you,' the couple were content and settled in.

As I too made myself comfortable again, I glanced around, startled to discover that the blonde was directly across the aisle. As I looked over, she met my gaze and said, 'Hi.' I was frozen; *she* was sat across from me, beautiful blue eyes and a gorgeous smile. All I could muster in return was a simple *hi* back, before our eyes parted company and focused elsewhere.

As the plane trundled along the ground preparing for takeoff, the old man beside me turned and offered me a sweet. 'I don't know about you but I always need these for the popping,' my bearded neighbour said, flashing a salesman's smile and pushing them towards me.

'Popping? What popping? This is my first flight,' I said quietly, hoping that the blonde wouldn't hear me, all the while feeling more and more nervous at what I was getting into.

'Your ears will pop with the pressure as we ascend. It's normal, just suck on the sweet,' he reassured.

I wasn't expecting the sudden burst of speed from the plane as it careered down the runway. The strange thing was that as soon we were up in the air and flying, it didn't feel as though we were moving at all, just being tilted at different angles. I tried not to look at how the lady at the window was faring but there was little else to focus on. She seemed okay though, completely transfixed on the world outside. I, on the other hand, was beginning to feel a little jittery as the plane began to shake.

'Turbulence,' the old man reassured me, obviously noticing me tighten my seatbelt. 'Close your mouth, pinch your nose shut and try to blow out - it'll also help with the popping,' he added, before giving me a quick demonstration. As I tried it out myself, I found it did work but only in my right ear, the left remained the same. I tried again, this time as hard as I could manage but still the left wouldn't ease up.

'It only works on one ear,' I told him.

'Did you blow as hard as you could?' he asked, stroking his trim beard of brown and silver hairs.

'Yeah, never mind. It's definitely helped,' I said, not wanting to be a nuisance, although I had the feeling his wife was going to stare out the window throughout the flight, leaving him keen for distractions.

When the in-flight entertainment was turned on I began pressing buttons on my television remote, only to discover that no matter what I tried nothing happened. Looking around, everyone else seemed to be working their own - everyone except the blonde, who was engrossed in a book. A few minutes went by, I fumbled through the in-flight magazines and tried the television again, but my mind was too fidgety.

'Where are you headed?' I asked, deciding to inflict my restlessness on someone else, as I turned to my left. Looking up from her book, with a smile, she folded the top corner of her page and gently closed it, placing it down on her lap.

'Bangkok... Is there another city the plane stops in?' she asked, mocking my question.

'Well no, I guess not. It's just that you could be... Oh forget it. I'm Matt,' I said, stretching out my hand across the aisle.

'Claire,' she said, stretching her hand out to meet my own. 'So, this is your first time on a plane then, Matt?'

'...Oh, you heard huh? Yeah, we always took family holidays in England or Wales. I must say, I'd imagined flying to be a bit more exciting,' I replied.

'Trust me, I've flown quite a few times, although never for this many hours but it's always a drag, even the quick flights. So how long are you on holiday for?' she asked.

'A year; I'm going to Thailand for three weeks, before flying down to Australia for the rest of the time. And you?'

'I've got just two weeks in Thailand before a few months in Oz. Not quite as long,' she smiled, 'I'm meeting my boyfriend Brent out there,' she added, knocking the wind out of my sails.

'Oh yeah?' I asked, trying to sound casually interested but I'd already started drifting away from the conversation.

'Brent's been in Sydney since July. As soon as university finished he flew out, leaving me alone for the summer,' her tone sounded slightly bitter but I dismissed it, thinking perhaps I'd been mistaken.

'So he's not going to Thailand for your first two weeks?' I asked, trying to act interested, but all I could now think about was my broken television.

'Oh God no. He wanted to though, but I really want to experience the independent backpacking thing, before I get thrust back into being with him again,' she said.

'I can understand that,' I answered, although I couldn't. Given the choice, I wouldn't be going solo but I wasn't about to tell the world about my insecurities. 'So, where are you actually heading to while you're in Thailand?' I asked, hopeful that we might cross paths.

'Well, I've got a couple of friends from uni who went to Thailand last summer and they told me about a full moon party on one of the islands... hang on a second, I've got the name written down somewhere,' Claire said before unzipping her small bag and producing a neatly folded piece of paper.

'Here it is…Koh Pha Ngan. My friends suggested spending a couple of days in Bangkok, just getting used to the heat and the food, before taking a bus down there. Then I reckon I'll spend a week on the island. The full moon is on the eleventh, so eight days from now I'll be there for that before heading back to Bangkok for some shopping and flying on to Sydney. What about you?' she asked.

'I'm staying in Thailand until the twenty-third of December, before flying over to Sydney to spend Christmas and New Year on Bondi Beach. The only place I'd worked out to go in Thailand was to one of the islands in the southwest, hopefully to try scuba diving, but beyond that I figured I'd wait until I arrived. Maybe I'll meet some other travellers, or something, like in that movie *The Beach*. Have you seen it?' I asked, then immediately regretted it, not wanting to seem like I was comparing my life to a movie.

'No, I heard it was rubbish. I read the book a few years ago though, that was good. So, which island is it, where you can scuba dive?' she asked.

'Um, it's one of the Koh's, not the one you mentioned though. Let me check,' I said, unclipping my seatbelt and reaching up for my *mellow* backpack from the overhead locker. Glancing inside brought a picture into my mind of both my Thailand and Australia guidebooks sitting on my bedside table, along with my travel alarm clock, which I'd also bought especially for the trip, none of which were in my bag. In particular, the Thailand guidebook had months' worth of notes and scribbles, as well as Lola's email address.

34

'*Shit*,' I mumbled to myself. 'Um, Claire you don't happen to have a Thailand guidebook, per chance?' I asked, as I put the bag back up and sat down, feeling a little flustered and embarrassed that I'd forgotten such an important thing.

'No sorry, I didn't think I'd need one,' she said with indifference.

'What? *Not need one*? Of course you'll need one, I mean how will you know where to stay and what to do?' I blurted, inwardly beginning to panic at my stupidity and Claire's flippant remark.

'Oh, I've already got that sorted,' she smugly replied.

'Oh, yeah I thought about booking a hotel beforehand too. Probably should have, in hindsight.'

'No, I haven't booked ahead, as I said before my friends were there last summer and they wrote down exactly where to stay and go. So, I didn't see the point in buying a book as well, not for just two weeks, maybe if I had a month or longer I would have.'

'Oh right, I'd worked out a good few possible places to go too but I had it all written in the book. So… where did your friends tell you to stay in Bangkok? Just out of curiosity, as I don't really know where to go now.'

'From my friend's instructions it seems as though we just need to jump on a bus outside the airport and it'll take us straight to some road or other, where there are about a hundred or so guesthouses and hotels, all for a few quid a night. So I'd say that would be your best bet, if you don't mind catching a bus with me that is?' Claire answered, with what I thought was a hopeful look.

'Khao San Road?' I asked. Thinking of *The Beach* and my own research into Bangkok.

'Yeah, that's it, I think.'

'Okay, cool, the bus would be good. Safety in numbers and all that,' I joked, as we broke out in nervous smiles and our conversation grounded to a comfortable silence.

Claire returned to her book and I fiddled again in vain with my television remote before giving up once and for all, deciding to try and get a little sleep. Woken up a while later with breakfast, I began tucking in when, without any warning, the plane began to violently shake causing me to spill orange juice across my lap. The *fasten seatbelts* sign flashed and the captain's voice echoed through the cabin, urging everybody to remain seated and buckled up.

Nervously, I looked over to seek reassurance from my bearded neighbour but he was a little too busy trying to calm down his wife.

With nowhere else to turn, I glanced over at Claire, who noticed my gaze and smiled 'Don't worry, it's just a little turbulence.'

'Turbulence *right*,' I replied, returning the smile before tightening my seatbelt a notch more and trying to focus my attention on the meal before me.

For the rest of the flight I tried to sleep, despite getting woken up by short periods of turbulence at which time I always shot Claire a glance for conversation to take my mind off it, only to find her either absorbed in her book or sleeping.

Following Claire out of the air-conditioned airport, the heat and humidity hit me. It was only five in the morning but I'd broken out into a light sweat by the time we'd walked the few paces to our bus. On top of the heat there was a spicy aroma that I couldn't put my finger on but which added to the tropical feel of my surroundings. That was until the air was suddenly filled by the pungent familiar smell of cigarettes, as Claire lit up, getting the nicotine fix she'd been craving.

The bus moved easily through the early morning traffic towards Khao San Road, the place I'd remembered the guidebook referring to as the backpackers' Mecca and a must on any trip through South-East Asia. Claire and I were in awe at the groups of Buddhist monks, the only sign of life on the morning streets, their saffron robes adding an intense colour to the dull grey pavements. Staring out through the grimy window and into the dawn light, I felt an incredible satisfaction wash over me. I was finally abroad. I could smell it, stretch out my hand and touch it - I'd really done it.

Khao San Road, from my memory of *The Beach*, was a bustling market place, full of mystery. But as we stepped off the bus and stood at the top of the road, it looked muted and worn out. I'd expected a twenty-four hour party street, where adventures began and ended. Oblivious to my dismay, Claire produced the piece of paper her friends had written on, instructing her to the best budget accommodation. However, after walking past a dozen guesthouses, in as many steps, it was clear that we were looking for a needle in a haystack. So, in an effort to put my bag down and get some sleep I suggested we just try the nearest one.

'Okay, *yeah*. They're probably all similar costs and the same inside, so why not,' she agreed, much to my surprise.

Heading up a flight of stairs under the strain of my luggage, I felt relieved that I was about to get a room and a bed to crash out on.

However, the small Thai lady behind the counter managed to deny my simple request.

'What, no rooms *at all*?' I pleaded, hoping I'd heard her wrong.

'No room,' she replied in simple English, with a friendly smile.

Five more guesthouses later and I was questioning my reasons for not having booked a hotel for the first few nights, before I left England. Guesthouse number seven, was called just that, '7'. It was Claire's turn to ask this time, catching her breath before speaking.

'Hello, do you have two rooms?' she asked a frail old man behind the reception who was glued to a small black and white television on the counter.

'Only one room,' the old man behind the reception replied.

'Er, no, we need two,' I repeated.

'Only have one,' he stressed. His transfixed gaze not leaving the screen.

'Okay, well you take it Claire,' I said, stepping aside like a gentleman.

'No, don't be silly Matt. How about we share it?'

'What are there two beds?' I asked her rather naively.

'One room. One bed,' the old man snapped.

'There's only one bed. You take it Claire,' I said, as I moved to pick up my bags.

'No, come on we're both tired, that's not fair on you, let's share.'

'What? You want to share a bed?' I questioned, not sure we were both talking about the same thing.

'We're both adults, I trust you. I'll have my side and you'll have yours, unless you'd rather spend the rest of the morning trying to find another room?' she shrugged.

'Okay, if you're sure, but no monkey business though, alright?' I said, hoping, of course, there would be.

The room was basic with no windows, except for a small area of mesh above our door leading out into the corridor. One double bed with a tired looking sheet, pockmarked with cigarette burns, a small table and most crucially, a rusty old fan bolted to the wall.

The sleeping arrangements seemed simple enough, pick a side, lie down and stay there. Although I had aspirations to do other than that, I knew nothing was going to happen. Apart from having a boyfriend, she was way out of my league. As tired as I was, I knew that rule number one of sharing a bed with a beautiful woman is: *be clean*. So I dug my towel and soap out of my backpack and headed for the door in search of a shower. Claire, however, had already made herself comfortable, stretched out across the middle of the bed.

'*Now* where are you going?' she asked, before I could leave.

'Er…shower. I really need one,' I replied, holding up my soap and towel.

'Nonsense, I stink, so you may as well stink too,' she said. With one hand on the door handle, I gave her words some thought before she added. 'Stop thinking and come to bed Matt,' it was all the persuading I needed, as she shuffled up a bit to the left to give me some space, although still taking up some of my side.

When I woke up, I lay for a moment staring up at the fan, embracing the light breeze that passed my face every few seconds. I could hear people out in the corridor going about their business and as I turned to see if I'd been imagining sharing a bed with Claire, it was empty, but she was stood on the other side of the room, wrapped in a pink towel, her blonde hair dripping water down onto the white tiled floor. Instinctively, I turned over trying to give her some privacy.

'What are the showers like?' I asked the wall.

'Cold but *very* refreshing. Hurry up and have one, then we can go and explore. I don't know about you, but I'm starving,' she replied.

The quiet road we'd arrived at only hours before, was now full of lunacy and chaos as we stepped out onto the bustling street. The pavements had been transformed into narrow alleyways with shops on one side and market stalls down the other. People were everywhere, backpackers, locals and oddballs, but it didn't matter as they all had their purpose, or so it seemed. Cars slowly edged their way down the road, honking their horns at the crowds uncaringly walking out into their paths. *This* was the Khao San Road I was expecting, which made me nervously excited.

Within minutes I was drenched in sweat, as a bright midday sun loomed over us, its power instantly undoing the efforts of the icy shower minutes before. The humidity was sapping my energy away with great speed as we walked from one end of the road to the other, stopping every few paces to see what was on sale. Although it soon became evident that it would be a harder search to find something that wasn't for sale, as everything from tailored suits to driving licenses were up for grabs.

Picking out a small restaurant for lunch, I was amazed to see that one of Hollywood's latest offerings was on show. Claire, on the

38

other hand, seemed to be expecting this and had just taken everything we'd seen since getting off the plane in her stride, making me wonder where I'd be right now, on my first day, without either her or my guidebook.

The menu was either variations of rice and noodle dishes or an overpriced western plate of chips. Having read about the various dodgy stomach upsets that plague travellers here, I decided on the chips, only to receive a scornful look from Claire.

'What?' I asked, not sure what I'd done wrong.

'*Matt*...Do you like noodles?'

'Yeah,' I replied, as though it was a stupid question.

'And do you like rice?'

'Yeah.'

'And curry?'

'Of course. Why?' I quizzed, unable to see where her twenty questions were headed.

'Well, if you like all these things, then *why* did you choose something you could have down the local chippy back in England? If you're going to fly half way around the world, you may as well eat the local food and learn something about the local way of life, don't you think?' she contended.

'But...but I read that you should be careful of what you eat, you know *Bangkok belly* and all that?' I argued, but it was a hopeless effort.

'So you're happy ordering some western imitation shit from here but you're worried that the locals won't be able to cook their own specialties properly, is that what you mean?' she continued and put like that I had little choice but to agree, as her words highlighted our difference in years and life experiences.

'Hmmm... Okay, well consider this my last bowl of chips until I get to Australia,' I replied, conceding to her point.

The movie blared in the background but went largely unnoticed between us, as Claire and I shared our first impressions and our plans for the next few days. Top of my list was to buy a new guidebook and follow my original plans. Claire's were still to head down to Koh Pha Ngan for the full moon party in a day or two. For the time being though neither of us had the energy to do much of anything but hide out in the shade and watch the busy world go by. Eventually, after what was at least three hours in the restaurant, we paid up and left. Although I'd sent my mum a text when we'd landed I knew she would be expecting a phone call, which I made while Claire headed off to email her boyfriend. My mum was in tears by the end of the call, finding it hard to come to terms that I was so far away, which pushed all thoughts of asking her to find Lola's email address out of my head. After hanging up I couldn't help but feel sad, as if I'd broken her heart by leaving. But with one look around at the choice I'd made, I felt any regrets quickly melt away, replaced by a buoyant feeling of great adventure and independence.

The heat was soon too intense for us both, forcing a cowardly retreat back into our room until the sun went down. We talked like old friends about our past few years, our families and our future hopes. As much as I tried to liven up my school years, they paled in comparison to Claire's university stories. I just hoped that in a year, Kermit's stories would look dull in comparison to my travel chronicles.

Claire also shared a few travel tips she'd picked up from her friends. She told me that if somebody was keen enough to rip us off they could and would and the best thing we could do was to keep our passports and airline tickets in the guesthouse safe and our wallets on us at all times. That way, losing a bag wouldn't be such a big problem. So, on our way out for dinner I handed in my passport with its lonely stamp inside.

New stalls were just setting up for a night of trading, and incredibly the road seemed even busier than in the day. Deciding not to sit in a movie house, we opted for a small and quieter place with some ambient tunes playing. The seating was a mixture of cushions on the floor and wooden deck chairs, with tables of varied heights. Taking the lead, Claire chose the cushions so I sat at the other side of the foot high table, facing Claire who was looking stunning, wearing a sky blue cotton dress, her blonde hair clipped back.

Again the menu had the three staple choices but this time I opted for a rice dish, having agreed to broaden my horizons earlier in the day.

'Do you always gel your hair like that?' Claire asked bluntly as she lit up a cigarette.

'Yeah, *why* what's wrong with it?' I asked defensively, feeling like I'd had my choices pulled apart a few times by Claire in the past few hours. It was clear she wasn't as impressed with me as I was with her.

'It's just that the gelled look really doesn't suit you. I think you'd look much better with it left naturally.'

'Naturally? It goes really curly like that, no way,' I protested. Ever since I had been old enough to care, I'd been gelling it down, trying my best to repress the natural spring.

'Okay, but I can guarantee you the ladies will like it better,' she remarked, hitting an obvious weak spot.

'*Really?*'

'Yeah, definitely, I know that I would prefer it,' she said, leaving the topic there for me to think about as her eyes turned to the waitress carrying our drinks.

The beer was a definite saviour throughout the meal, as the strong local spices caught me off guard, although the food tasted great, much better than the bland chips I'd opted for at lunch. Long after my mouth had cooled down, the beer was still disappearing quickly between us and as we drunkenly made our way through the still busy street, Claire moved in closer and put an arm through mine linking us together. After that, the walk back was made in silence, as we studied the world around us and tried to find our guesthouse among the hundreds of others.

A little while later, I was back lying on the right side of the bed, a foot of thin air away from Claire. In my intoxicated state, I began to wish that I wasn't sharing a bed, as I didn't want to make a drunken move, which would ruin our friendship. So, given the situation, it seemed that the best thing to do was get some sleep and prepare for the inevitable head pounding hangover. I also had no doubt that across the bed Claire was wishing that lying beside her was her rugby-playing boyfriend.

After a good ten minutes spent trying to sleep, I was lying on my side facing the wall and trying my best to block out all thoughts of Claire, when I heard her move. Pretending to be asleep I froze.

'Matt?' she whispered.

'Yeah?' I tried to sound weary, like I'd just been rudely woken up.

'I can't sleep. It's too hot,' she moaned.

'Me neither. Should we go back out to a bar?' I asked as I turned over to face her, knowing that the window above the door lit the room up well enough to see each other. As I made eye contact she just smiled and slowly leant in and kissed me. It wasn't a long passionate kiss, more of a stunted one made by two guilty teenagers. As she pulled back I looked into her eyes for an indication of whether or not there was regret or worse still, disgust. Instead I saw a familiar smile, as she shuffled across shrinking the gap down to only a couple of inches.

Five minutes later I was up out of bed and throwing the contents of my *mellow* bag across the room. Somewhere inside were the condoms that the guys had given me, but in my moment of need in the dingy light they were eluding me and I was afraid that Claire's waiting body had a time limit that was about to expire any second.

That first night in Bangkok went on forever, as we ended up entangled in each other. I lay awake in a sweaty mess, listening to Claire's slow deep breathing as my mind raced with new possibilities for my travel plans. I wanted to wake up Claire and ask her whether she felt we had a future together beyond Bangkok. If she said yes, then we could celebrate the full moon together and then meet up again in Australia as soon as she'd gotten rid of her boyfriend. This plan would, of course, mean I'd fail at my challenge set by Ben and the others, but as far as I could see she was more than worth losing it for. After what felt like hours later, my mind finally stopped running through the different scenarios and I found sleep, my first day aboard came to an end.

Running my tongue around my mouth and over my dry lips, I could still taste the previous night's beer in my breath and Claire's strawberry flavoured chapstick on my lips. Judging by the noise from the corridor, our guesthouse had woken up, and the morning had arrived. The reality of the night's actions began to filter into my mind. It had all seemed great with alcohol fuelling us both, but I knew it would all be different now, with the sobriety of the morning and not necessarily for the better. I for one, didn't wish for our relationship to step back again to its platonic beginnings, but it wasn't entirely my decision and without a doubt there would be an air of awkwardness to follow.

In the night Claire had moved back to her side of the bed, her hand still remaining across my stomach. Leaning off the bed a little, I managed to reach a bottle of water and as I quenched my thirst I felt Claire's hand move off my stomach. Glancing over at her, she was lying naked, peering out at me through tired eyes.
'Morning. Water?' I meekly asked, trying to prevent the uncomfortable tension that I felt was sure to build up.
'Oh, thanks,' she replied in a friendly voice, taking the bottle off me, but making no effort to cover up.
Staring at the nicotine-stained ceiling, I watched out of the corner of my eye as Claire stood up, wrapped a towel around her body

and disappeared out of the door, without so much as a kiss or another word. As soon as the door closed I too stood up and threw on my shorts, unsure where I was going but knowing I needed to get out of the stuffy room.

Outside, the sun was shining brightly and the temperature was already in the thirties. The road was bustling and for a moment, I toyed with the idea of doing a runner. If there was going to be an uncomfortable tension between us now, I didn't want to stay and suffer it. Squinting in the morning sky, I knew I'd have to go back upstairs and face the consequences. If it meant we were now going our separate ways then so be it, but I did need to get a quick picture of her on my phone to send back home and knock down the first part of the challenge.

Climbing back up the three flights of stairs, Claire was already back in the room, towelling off, 'what are you doing? Hurry up and have a shower,' she instructed, 'and be quick, I'm starving,' she added as I grabbed my towel and soap, dashing back out of the door. All the while I was trying to analyse what she'd said, how she'd said it and what it might mean.

My wet hair dripped down onto the bare restaurant table, as I waited for a banana pancake, hoping that Claire would notice I'd followed her suggestion to keep my hair natural. But if she had, she wasn't letting on. Food wise, it became clear that breakfast was a good time for western style food, as rice and noodles so early in the day had already lost its appeal for both of us. Especially as we knew there would be plenty of both later.

'So… last night?' I began. 'What are… ?' but I was stopped in my mentally rehearsed speech, as Claire's face turned serious and she butted in.

'Last night was *fun*. And if you want, then tonight can be too. I mean, I like you Matt, and I know you feel the same so why shouldn't we have a little sex? While we're here, we're both single and free. So why not?' Claire bluntly stated, as though reconfirming a business deal, but it wasn't enough for me I still had questions.

'What about when we get to Australia?' I asked. 'What about your boyfriend Bret?'

'His name is *Brent* and he's *in* Australia, which means that I'm free to enjoy the independent backpacking thing. When I get to Australia, there is no you and I though Matt, *only Brent and I.* Is that clear?' she said, jabbing her fork aggressively towards me to drive her point home.

'Until then...' she continued, 'you should come to the full moon party with me, since you're not sure which island it was that you were headed for.'

'What about the whole *independent backpacking thing*, I mean I don't want to spoil your fun?' I replied, suddenly feeling less enthusiastic about the whole arrangement, as she tried to dictate my plans.

'Don't worry about that, as long as I'm away from Brent I'm doing my own thing. He's a little controlling and constantly suspicious that I'm playing away, so I need times like this away from him without any of his hassles,' she said, sending alarm bells off in my head.

'I can't possibly see why he would think such a thing,' I sarcastically offered. 'Why are you still with him if he's like that?'

'Like what?' she asked, clearly a little uncomfortable with the question.

'Controlling?' I offered.

'Because I love him, *look*, can we stop talking about Brent please?' she snapped, before calming down and repeating her invitation. 'So are you coming to the full moon party with me tomorrow or not?'

'Where you from? What's your name? You see something you like? Maybe you buy?' The same constant questioning in Bangkok and I was more than ready to head to a beach. The novelty had really worn off after the second day, which had largely been spent shopping. I'd enjoyed haggling over my first purchase of a tattered guidebook, but every seller asked you the same questions and by the end of the day everything was just too intense and tiring.

In the evening of the third day, we arrived at the tiny gift shop front that our travel agents called their *office*. Waiting around for twenty minutes, expecting to see a horde of other travellers congregate before the bus pulled up, there was no evidence of them, the bus or the agent who had sold us the ticket. Five minutes after our supposed departure time, I walked into the gift shop looking for reassurance that the bus would come. As I asked the small woman sat behind the counter, she looked at me blankly before turning to a larger stern looking lady, who immediately snatched our tickets out of my hand and began yelling in Thai at her colleague, occasionally stopping to point at me. I peered out of the shop looking for help from Claire, who was busy delving in the bottom of her bag trying to find her lighter.

44

Without warning, tickets in hand, the large lady sprang into action waddling towards the exit with a pace that defied her heavy body. As she reached the doorway, she paused to look at me and snapped. 'Okay, follow now,' before darting out of the door. Still in a world of her own, Claire stood peering up and down the road, as I dashed out and grabbed my bags. 'Come on!' I yelled as I began to tear off after the lady. Glancing back, I could see Claire was in pursuit, struggling to run in flip-flops, under the weight of her bag. The agent weaved in and out of the crowds with surprising grace, whilst we, on the other hand, knocked, bashed and pushed our way through the crowds desperately trying to keep up.

As she darted down a narrow alleyway to the left, we stuck to her like glue, myself a dozen paces behind and Claire even further back. As we followed unquestioningly through the labyrinth of alleyways, I started to worry about how a bus would fit down one of these alleys and began to panic that we were being lured into a trap. She still had our tickets though and so putting a little faith in her intentions, desperation kept my legs going as we continued to give chase.

The buildings down these alleys were different to the ones on the main road. There was a strong smell in the air that appeared to be a mix of faeces and spices. One building we passed was made out of wood, standing defiantly among the others of stone, but with a slight slant, as if it was desperately trying to stay upright just to keep the memories of the old days alive. Then, the pathway widened, and we were back out near a main road buzzing with cars and tuk tuks. On our left we could see three big buses, all displaying the letters 'VIP' on their windscreens. Our agent ground to a halt at the first one, and looking at us with real disdain, bent double as she heaved air into her lungs. As I tried to offer her some water, she ignored it and pushed our tickets back into my hand, before slowly hobbling away. By this point we were both drenched in sweat and eager to sit down and relax. However, as we tried to board, we realised she'd taken us to the wrong bus; ours next to it, was slowly starting to pull out as I jumped in front, waving the tickets like a demented fool.

The twelve hours flew by, as we drove through the night, comfortably reclined on the airline style seats and wrapped up in a complementary blanket. Every few hours, chaotic toilet breaks showed glimpses of another Thailand. Opening the toilet door I noticed two things - a sickening smell and instead of a toilet there was a hole in the ground with grooved foot shaped areas on either side of the void. I'd read about these squat toilets, although the relative luxury of Bangkok's tourist area had caused me to forget about them. Now, trying hard not to step in the wrong places, I began to curse my decision to wear flip-flops. Standing precariously over the rancid gap, my nose and stomach were waging an internal war with the stench.

Moments later, savouring the fresher air outside I made my way back to the bus, only to realise I had no idea which one was mine or what my driver looked like. The six buses parked up all claimed VIP status and looked the same. Cautiously I poked my head in what I guessed to be the right one, when I felt a sharp pain in my arse cheek.
'What the fu…?' I yelped, feeling a poke and hitting my elbow on the door, turning to see what had jabbed at me.
'Where are you going?' Claire asked with a curious look.
'I'm getting on the bus,' I defiantly said, trying to hide any doubt I had that this was our bus.
'Oh, okay, well I'll see you later then I guess, *my* bus is over there,' she merrily pointed out, glancing over at an identical vehicle.
'I know that. Duh, I was just going to have a look to see if there was anyone I knew on this one first,' I lied, as I turned and followed Claire towards our waiting chariot.

After the road journey, we had an unscheduled two-hour wait for the ferry in a tiny café, with overpriced crap food that reminded me of the service stations back home. It was during this time, spent sat around picking at a bowl of bland noodles, that I noticed the sounds of humming and buzzing insects all around us, hidden but watchful, within the surrounding trees. The surrounding landscape was green and lush with huge palms dotting the tree line, reminding me of the tropical surf videos I had watched which had fuelled my dreams of a faraway paradise.

When we finally got moving again after boarding the ferry, I just wanted to sleep, but a handful of hotel touts were walking around trying to persuade every foreigner to choose their accommodation. One of them was a born salesman and after hearing his little spiel and seeing a few pictures, I was sold. Claire, on the other hand, was uninterested in anything he or I had to say, determined to stick with her plan. At least now we had a guidebook and although it didn't mention any of the guesthouses on Claire's list, we knew which part of the island we were headed to.

The squashed taxi ride was shared with a dozen other backpackers, all squatting in the back of a pickup truck, holding on tight to the sides, as we raced from the port towards the village of Hat Rin Nok. Despite the driver's best efforts to kill us all with breakneck speeds around scary hairpin bends and down steep hills, we reached our destination unscathed and instantly the beauty of the island bay came into view. Banking green cliffs on either side of the golden sand and a scatting of small boats moored in the turquoise water, it looked postcard perfect.

Despite our exhaustion from the trip, Claire opted to hunt around and find the places her friends had recommended. Finding one, after a twenty-minute slog through the village, we were amply rewarded. Individual bungalows were scattered about the hillside at the northern end of the village, each room commanding stunning views out to the sparkling sea.

Four

Lying in my new hammock, stretched across our private balcony with uninterrupted views of the bay, life felt very good. Although a mosquito buzzing around my ear was attempting to ruin the ambience. I couldn't see the pest, but I could hear it every few seconds as it flew past an ear, searching for a tasty bit of exposed flesh. With every grab at thin air I made, the insect would fall silent for a moment, making me believe I'd got it, before resuming. For a moment I considered getting up and lighting a mosquito coil beneath the hammock, but I could sense that the sea breeze would just blow the smoke away without helping my situation.

Hearing Claire coming out of the bedroom, I turned my head in time to see her hand swiping towards my face, narrowly missing, but making me sit up, puzzled by her actions.

'Got it and it got you, look at all that blood,' she proudly announced, holding up her bloodied palm, before wiping it on the outside of the hammock and squeezing in beside me.

'Do you want to go for a swim?' I asked, as I could feel another itch starting on my ankle but fought the compulsion to move and scratch it. In the past few hours, I'd been bitten at least a dozen times and my body was beginning to become one big scratching post.

'Nah, I just want to relax and do some reading, don't you have a book to read so that you can chill out a little?' Claire replied, opening her novel. It was the third time I'd tried to get her swimming since we'd arrived and each time she passed, which meant I hadn't gone either.

'No, I'm not really much of a reader,' I answered, before getting up out of the hammock, leaving her swinging.

'Where are you going?' she asked, peering up over the side.

'Swimming,' I said, digging through my backpack for my board shorts.

'If you wait a couple of hours I'll come with you.'

'I'll go swimming again in a couple hours too if you like, but right now I need to get wet,' I called, before darting out of the room.

'Bye then,' she grumpily called out as I left.

The seawater was like a bath and after stroking away from the shore for a few minutes, I turned back to the beach for a panoramic view. It certainly looked a lot less spectacular than it had from our room. On my swim out I'd passed various fragments of litter floating about and now, glancing back towards the shore, I could see that the sand was packed with bodies, with an unbalanced mixture of bar after bar lining the village and only a few tall palm trees in between. Hardly the tropical paradise I had in mind.

Despite being some distance from the shore I could hear music emanating from the bars, and in an instant I could suddenly imagine the party being a fierce competition between the different bars, all striving for the loudest sounds and the most revellers. Feeling disappointed at the scene before me, I began to swim back, wondering if maybe I had stumbled upon the wrong party. This I could get in a nightclub. I wanted something more chilled, like the beach party I'd experienced in Newquay, sat around a fire with a few spliffs and a drum.

Reaching the shallows, I decided that if it meant staying with Claire for a few more days, I'd stay. After all, I was here for new experiences and it was certainly going to be just that.

I reflected on the past five days since leaving England, which had raced by. The journey had, so far, been everything I'd hoped for and more. After all I had already had sex, which meant I only had to find two more conquests before the morning of New Year's Day, although I had yet to take a picture of Claire. Sex aside, though, befriending Claire was undoubtedly the best start I could have hoped for. She more than made up for my naivety. There was no doubt in my mind that I was doing the right thing backpacking, I just wasn't sure if I was backpacking in quite the right place.

A warm, breezeless, night crept upon us and my mind finally began to relax after the initial few days of culture shock induced stress. Heading out for dinner and taking a slow walk through the busy village, there seemed to be more than double the number of travellers that I'd seen on the beach earlier in the afternoon. The main stretch of shops and bustling restaurants mirrored Khao San Road, except that this road was made of mud, with huge puddles dotted about.

'This is so busy. I thought we were heading to a tiny island with just a few people here, like the tropical islands you see in the movies, you know?' I admitted, as I felt the splatter of mud hit the back of my leg, jettisoned from my flip-flops.

'*Christ Matt*, wake up. This is Thailand and what's more this is full moon party time. If you think this is busy wait a day or two until the big night. I personally think this is cool, people from so many different backgrounds all coming here to celebrate together and lose their inhibitions for a night on drink and drugs,' she happily argued, obviously enjoying the busy vibe that flowed through the village.

'*Drugs*? *Yeah right*? Getting caught here means a death penalty or life in some dodgy prison, eating cockroaches. There's no way anyone's going to risk that and do drugs here,' I stated.

'Oh, you *are* naive Matt, of course they will and so will I. Although I'm not so sure about the ecstasy here, I might just stick to diet pills or something a little safer,' she said, with knowledgeable authority.

'*Diet Pills*?' I quizzed, eyeing up her already slim waistline.

'Yeah, they increase your metabolism and kind of work like speed, means I can dance all night until the sun comes up. You fancy it?' she asked.

'Well, call me old fashioned, but I figured I might just stick with beer, at least until I get to Australia and don't need to worry about rotting in a prison for skinning up,' I argued, as Claire threw me a look of disappointment, as if I'd just gone down a notch in her opinion.

The day of the full moon party came around quickly, and as Claire had predicted the masses of people had already trebled in the past days. The past couple of days had been spent relaxing in the hammock, on the beach, in bars and taking the occasional swim in the litter-strewn sea. My pasty English complexion was diminishing fast, only visible beneath my baggy shorts and flip-flop straps.

The more time we spent together, the stronger my feelings for Claire became and I couldn't help but feel a twinge of jealously each time she went to email Brent. Although I felt this was in part because every time I checked my emails, I had nothing but spam. Sending daily updates to my friends back home was beginning to seem fruitless. I'd expected to get a response to my announcement that I was already a third of my way through the challenge, but there was nothing.

As we counted down the hours to the big party, we decided to head down to the beach to top up our tans. Claire had given me her old book and so, laying down on a couple of her sarongs, we got comfortable under the sweltering sun.

'Are you thirsty Matt?' Claire asked a little while later, not looking up from her book.

'A little yeah. Did you bring the water?' I replied, with a sneaking suspicion where this was heading.

'No, I thought you did, but clearly not. Would you mind getting some?' she asked. Pausing for a moment, I put my book down and glanced around, looking for the closest shop and realising it was going to have to be a trip to the main road. 'Okay, sure,' I conceded, pulling myself up from the hot ground and checking my pockets for a few baht.

Dodging in and out of sunbathers and strolling past a beach volleyball court, I made my way onto the main road and ducked into the first shop I came across. Walking back a minute later, I noticed two guys sitting down on the sand, chatting with Claire. Envy ran through me, as I watched the three of them erupt into laughter. Strolling back as casually as possible, I purposely ignored the guys, as I resumed my position on the sarong next to Claire.

The two strangers sounded Scouse and introduced themselves as Dan and Gavin. Dan looked the youngest of the pair, although still a few years older than me. He had an immaculately trimmed goatee and long blond hair, slicked back. Wearing only a pair of Liverpool football shorts, his upper body was conditioned but hardly any more muscular than my own. Next to him, Gavin had a more thug like appearance with a large tattoo of a British Bulldog draped in a Union Jack flag on his right bicep and a small gold hoop in his right ear, below a freshly shaven head. He was stockier, with a protruding beer gut peering over his Nike shorts. Beyond the introduction they ignored me and switched their attention back to Claire, who seemed less agitated by their presence.

'So, what? Seven-thirty or eight?' Dan asked Claire.

'Sounds good Dan, you'll come and find us right?' Claire replied, to which Dan gave Claire a wink and he and Gavin walked away. As soon as they were out of earshot, I handed the water to Claire and waited for an explanation.

'Thanks Matt,' she said, taking a drink before turning over onto her front.

'So what's happening at eight?' I asked, prompting her to tell me what we were doing with them at eight.

'We're meeting up with them,' she curtly answered before turning away.

'*Them*? Do you even *know them*?' I questioned, an aggressive tone creeping into my voice as I waited for the full story.

'Matt, please don't start getting controlling, I have enough of that with Brent. They're our neighbours; I met them this morning whilst you were sleeping off your hangover. They're going to sort us out with drugs for tonight.'

'Sort *you* out, you mean,' I replied.

'*Whatever*,' Claire mumbled bringing our conversation to an end.

The rest of the afternoon was spent apart, as I retreated back to the hammock and slept while Claire remained on the beach. It was the first time we'd spent more than a few minutes apart and I was beginning to think that it might be time for me to head off as soon as the party was over.

As the sun began to set, Claire made her way back up to the room, giving me a kiss as she passed. It felt empty though and at once my mind was made up to head off the following morning. So picking up my guidebook, I tried to find the island I had originally planned to head for, with plans to pick up where I'd left off on the plane before teaming up with Claire.

As eight o'clock rolled around, Claire and I sat out in the hammock, hand in hand, waiting for Dan and Gavin to come around. Ready for a night of dancing, Claire's hair was tied up and she was wearing a green sarong and a white vest top, which she'd bought earlier that day. Dressed in shorts and a t-shirt as always, I decided to hold off telling Claire of my new travel plans until the morning, rather than ruining the night.

Twenty minutes late, Dan turned up alone, looking a little edgy. Flashing a nervous smile at us, he passed a small bag of pills into Claire's hands, taking a bundle of notes in the transaction.

'Great, thanks. Anything else you need?' he asked, causing Claire to turn to me in anticipation. Swallowing hard, I thought again of rotting away in a dingy cell and stood my ground, slowly shaking my head.

'Okay, well... enjoy,' Dan said before he disappeared into the night, signalling that it was time for us to go and join the party.

Before we left, Claire washed a few pills down with some water and put the rest in her little purse. 'I understand your reasons for not taking pills but you can't just drink beer tonight though Matt, you won't last the course,' she told me.

'I'll be alright,' I answered, thinking back to nightclubs at home.

'No, no you won't. I don't want you passing out bladdered after a couple of hours. 'Why don't you drink buckets tonight?' she asked, clutching my hand tighter as we descended the steps towards the beach. We'd seen people drinking buckets the previous evenings, and found out it consisted of a small plastic seaside bucket filled with a can of coke, a small bottle of Red Bull and a flask of whiskey mixed together and drunk through a straw.

'What and a bucket is meant to stop me getting drunk?' I questioned, thinking that it sounded quite lethal.

'It'll get you happy drunk and hopefully give you the stamina to keep up with me,' she explained before stopping and looking in my eyes, 'Matt, I want to enjoy this special night with you, but I'm not going to sacrifice my fun if you aren't on the same level as I am. If you're not going to take the pills then the least you can do is drink buckets.'

'Okay fine,' I conceded, as the music on the beach suddenly went up ten notches.

On the beach, disco lights were flashing out towards the sea. The thumping bass was resonating through us, making our bodies vibrate and the entire sandy beach had turned into a giant dance floor, already full of ravers. Making a beeline for a makeshift beach bar, I ordered a bucket, knowing that I needed to show Claire my commitment to the evening. After all my fears surrounding the concoction, I was a little disappointed to find it tasted just like a super sweet whiskey and coke. Hardly the crazy drink I'd built up in my mind.

Looking up and down the busy beach, we could see a small group of people twirling balls of fire around their bodies. Their bodies moved and swayed in tune to the nearby music, all the while the flames swung about them with perfect accuracy and rhythm. 'I tried that once, it's called poi,' Claire whispered to me.

'It looks pretty good,' I said, feeling hypnotised by the twirling light, before I felt my hand being jerked which pulled me sideways, 'Come on Mr Bucket,' she giggled, as I was led towards a different sound system.

Minutes later as we began to dance I sucked away at the bucket, watching Claire as the pills began to take a hold of her. She was getting lost in the music and I still wasn't quite there, so I speeded up my drinking trying to get to a similar place. Another two buckets later and I was feeling good. I could feel the alcohol's grip but I also felt awake and alive, starting to relax and really enjoy the evening for the first time. It was at that point that the evening peaked and suddenly, shrouded by the drunken mist, it began to spiral down out of control.

Claire shouted that she would be back, signalling something with her purse, which I took as a sign she was off to pop more pills. I didn't mind though, as I was happy for a break from the endless dancing and so wandered off for a quiet spot on the beach to take a breather. En route, I picked up another bucket and plonked myself down on the cold sand. As I gazed out to sea, I noticed for the first time that the waterline had inadvertently become a giant toilet. Guys were lined up all the way along the shore urinating into the dark sea. Thinking of the swim I took in the same water just hours before, I began to feel a little sick, not from the drink but the callousness of my fellow backpackers who gave no thought to the environment they'd come to enjoy.

Turning away from the sea in disgust, I began to scan the crowd for Claire. Bodies were everywhere, bouncing, twirling, moving with the pulsating beat. There was no way to determine where I'd just come from and every face belonged to a stranger. Getting up to have a walk around, but finding it hard to walk straight, I realised my bucket needed refilling, I needed another energy boost to keep me going.

I kept up my search for Claire as I swerved and pushed my way through an endless sea of moving bodies, my eyes focused on finding the blonde ponytail I knew so well. As I sucked up my fifth bucket, my mind was suddenly bombarded with negativity. I began to realise I was lost, no longer sure if I was looking in the right bar, they'd all blended into one and images flooded my mind of Claire dancing with another guy, one with stamina and pills in his system.

It was a fruitless search because I was wasted, that much I knew for certain. Not only that, but the buckets weren't having their desired effect. Instead of being full of energy all I wanted to do was sit down, stop moving and throw up. The latter came first but no one seemed to notice. I staggered away from the crowd, tripping over and part crawling until I reached the peaceful dark end of the beach, away from the flashing lights and the constant dancing. Retching again, I had a flash of hope that I could return to the party before the darkness completely enveloped me.

A brush against my leg woke me up. As I opened my tired eyes and looked around me, taking a moment to get my bearings, I realised it was an actual brush that had run against my bare shin. The golden sand was being swept by a young Thai girl who towered above me yet completely ignored my presence, as she cleaned the beach. Sitting up, startled, I tried desperately to comprehend where I was and what was happening. The sun was already up and I could now feel its warmth.

54

Music was still pumping out a hundred yards away and where there had been thousands of revellers on the beach, there now remained just a few dozen who were still dancing. As I tried to take everything in, my stomach heaved and I threw up on the warm sand, next to another, older splash of vomit.

Lying back down and curling into the foetal position, in an effort to ease my stomach pain, I closed my eyes willing my situation to all be a dream. I wanted to wake up back in my own bed at my mum and dad's, where I could stagger downstairs for a cup of tea and suffer in familiar surroundings. Either that, or to wake up in bed with Claire. The situation I was in was all too real though, my raw mouth tasted of sick, my head throbbed and the exposed parts of my arms and legs were cooking from the powerful sun that loomed above.

Finally getting the courage to sit up again, I remained frozen for another couple of minutes, before pushing up onto my feet and staggering across the beach. The hot sand beneath my feet was telling me that I'd lost my flip-flops, but I couldn't face turning back to look for them, scared that I would undo the progress I'd achieved. Through squinting eyes the sea sparkled and looked ever so inviting but as I plotted a course towards it, unsure whether I wanted to swim or drown, a flashback of hundreds of guys lined up pissing along the shoreline popped into my head, causing my stomach to heave and my legs to collapse beneath me.

It was slow and painful progress, but an eternity later I was making my way up the steps to the bungalow. The door was thankfully ajar and a nearly full bottle of water still sat on the bedside table. In one fluid motion I picked it up and collapsed across the bed, taking a few gulps of water before blacking out.

It was a few hours later before I woke up again. The fan was off and the air inside the room was stale. Moving, I could feel that the mattress was wet around my torso. In horror, I moved a hand down to my shorts, wondering how I would explain the accident to Claire, but they were dry and my bladder at bursting point. Curious, I sat up faster than I should have, with my head spinning furiously. I was relieved to discover the cause of the damp patch was the bottle of water, which I'd discarded on the bed as I'd passed out.

The nausea had passed and as I peered outside for Claire, I noticed that the lock on our door was splintered and was hanging loosely from the frame. Trying to recall if I'd done that, or Claire, it was then that I noticed most of my clothes and belongings scattered around the dusty tile floor of the bungalow. I was messy, but not that untidy and again I tried to cast my memory back to the events of the previous night, but nothing relevant came into focus. As I attempted to pick up a few things and clear the floor a little, it dawned on me that Claire's belongings were gone.

'*Shit*,' I murmured to myself. '*Shit*,' I repeated, trying to make sense of the situation. Claire's stuff was gone, mine was scattered, the door was broken. 'Okay, get a grip Matt. Claire came back couldn't get in, broke down the door, found I wasn't here and decided to leave,' as I listened to myself say the words, they didn't seem right. 'Or, I came back last night in a drunken stupor, couldn't get in, broke down the door, threw my clothes around the room, then threw Claire's stuff out before heading back down the beach for a sleep. *What the fuck*? Or... we were out, as everyone was last night, someone came and broke the door down, scattered my stuff around and nicked Claire's,' it still didn't seem quite right, but it was certainly more believable than picturing either myself or Claire shouldering the door in, when we both had keys.

Pottering around the room for another minute, thinking of different scenarios, the answer suddenly hit me, '*drugs*,' I whispered, 'fuck they were after drugs. The police must have known Claire had bought the drugs, broke in while we were out, searched our stuff, found something in her bag, taken it for evidence and arrested her at the party,' as I played my words over again and again in my head it all began to make sense, that was why she didn't come back, she'd been arrested. 'And that was why Dan was looking so edgy, he must have suspected someone was onto him, maybe... just maybe his mate had been arrested already, which is why he wasn't there and Dan was just trying to offload everything he had left, make enough money to leave the island.' The moment I said it, I knew it was true, it all fitted together like a jigsaw and I, the last piece, had to get off the island while I still could.

As I walked into the bathroom, to splash water on my face, I was beginning to panic. Claire had been arrested for drugs, her possessions taken. How long would it be until she sold me out and tried to rope me into the mess? I knew just one thing, I had to leave, and I had to leave immediately. Suddenly, my hangover was gone, my legs steadied and my headache was no longer a concern as adrenalin flooded my veins.

Stripping off my vomit splattered clothes, I jumped under the cold shower, in and out in seconds, before throwing on some clean clothes and stuffing everything else in the backpack. As I began a final check of the room, to make sure I had everything, I suddenly began to feel sick. Not from the alcohol this time though, perching on the edge of the bed to steady myself, my gaze was fixed on my big backpack and the lack of my small bag sat next to it. My *mellow* bag was gone. Gone like Claire and her bags. The contents weren't too important, my ipod, guidebook, cards and a packet of unopened cookies. Thankfully, my flight tickets were in my big backpack, wallet still in my pocket and passport in the guesthouse safe. It was more the principle of the matter, *they had my bag* and I was fucked if I was going to try and get it back from the police.

My best bet was to stick to the original plan, the route I'd mapped out the night before. Claire didn't know where I was headed and I had nothing left to stick around for. From the moment I stood back up, I felt like I was in automatic mode. I handed my key back, settled up, grabbed my passport, found a travel agent, booked a bus, took the ferry, caught the bus, took another ferry and finally that evening, without eating a single mouthful of food, I was where I was meant to be. Where I was meant to have been in the first place, Koh Phi Phi, a great spot for diving, across the coast from the full moon police, back on track, no questions asked, no lies told.

Five

Shuffling off my second boat of the journey and stepping onto Koh Phi Phi island, I began to feel better than I had all day. My belly was starting to hurt from hunger and I could still taste vomit in my arid mouth but none of that mattered, I had arrived. For every two small steps I took towards the lights of the centre, I was getting pushed back onto the boat by a horde of locals trying to board, loading it up with bulky items of cargo for its return voyage to the mainland.

I had no idea where I was going but evidently other backpackers, guidebooks in hand, did, so I picked a couple who looked friendly enough and followed them, keeping a few silent steps behind as we walked off the rickety old wooden pier and into the main village.

The further we walked the more the village began to resemble a labyrinth, with narrow alleys sprouting off in every direction. The couple, thankfully, seemed to know where they were going and so led by the map in their book, we all trudged on. The notion of having found my ideal chilled island was being stripped away as I realised the village in Koh Phi Phi was a bigger version of Hat Rin Nok but there were subtle differences. The people themselves and the restaurants all seemed a little less glitzy and less pretentious. This was, I reminded myself, an island that had had to rebuild itself after the devastating tsunami a few years before and perhaps as a result it had become a little more humble than its more famous cousin.

As we turned yet another a corner, past a crumbled old building, I felt like I'd twisted and turned so many times along the paths that I'd never find the dock again. Then ahead of us I saw the alleyway opening, the streetlights ended and we were in a small bay. Under the illumination of the bright moon, I could see high cliffs at each side and towering palms swaying over the sand. No bars, clubs or restaurants. This was the place I had imagined, closer to the images in the surf movies that I had studied so intensely.

As we continued along the sand the couple finally clicked that I was following and they turned around and smiled, seemingly under the impression that it was a happy coincidence we were all headed for the same place. When moments later we arrived, I breathed a sigh of relief that their taste in accommodation was just as I'd hoped. Set back from the beach was a guesthouse with a number of small bungalows dotted about a spacious garden. The price was almost three times the amount I had paid in Hat Rin Nok, but I would have gladly paid another ten times that price for the opportunity to stop and sleep.

That night I awoke in a feverish sweat, my mind ravaged by a nightmare. It was the horse again but this time he had a heavy chain around his neck, and shackles above his hooves. As he struggled to move, he found himself stuck to the spot, which had become a small grimy concrete room, before the horse suddenly became Claire. Not the young Claire I knew, but an older one, her youth and beauty gone, blue eyes hollow and vacant, her blonde hair dirty and matted. Her face was all I could see each time I closed my eyes as I lay under the breeze of my ceiling fan, weighing up whether I should go to the police, risk my own imprisonment as an accomplice to try and help Claire, or whether I should cut my losses and head home, pretending none of this had happened. Deep down though I knew I was overreacting to a bad situation, made worse by the still night air and as the morning light came, sure enough, it chased my demons away.

As slow as the night had been to leave, the day seemed in haste to retreat, as I spent my hours wandering around the village making a mental map of the layout, buying another guide book, swimming out in the shallow turquoise waters of the bay, trying to strike up conversation with my fellow travellers only to find my throat clenched, tongue frozen and mind blank. Returning to my room once again in the dark, I lay wide-awake trying to put off seeing Claire's gaunt face again, pushing it out with happier thoughts of home for as long as I could.

On my second morning in Koh Phi Phi, I had an overwhelming urge to hear some news from home and check my email for the first time in days. There was still nothing from Ben but I was elated to find a message from Kermit giving me a little of his gossip from university and a congratulations on achieving a third of my challenge, something I'd completely given up on. As uplifting as his email was, it still left me wanting. I needed something from home, to know it was still there, unchanged and it didn't matter whether it was from Ben or my family. Due to the time difference it was hours until I could phone home, so I did all I could for information, finding my town's local newspaper website and absorbing every word.

When hours later I did call home, there was no answer. Ten minutes later, after a brisk walk up and down the lane, I tried again, still no answer. Trying to think of reasons why my parents might not be at home, my mind constructed a number of horrific and unlikely scenarios - the house had burnt down, Rachel had been in a car crash, a bomb had exploded and someone had died. Whatever the scenario, I kept coming up with the fact that I needed to fly back home and it occurred to me that in the morning I could head back to Bangkok and catch the next flight home. Within 72 hours I'd be back to deal with the crisis.

So, as the evening had suddenly become my last on the island, I decided to take a last walk around the village and enjoy a final beer for the trip. Entering the first bar I came across, I didn't even make it five steps inside before turning around and walking away. It was the sort of bar I'd have loved back home. One of my favourite bands was blaring through the speakers, but it was full of people and more importantly, they were happy people. This beer wasn't meant to be a happy one. I craved a quiet pint in a quiet country pub, or as close as I could get, nearly six thousand miles away from such a haven.

Another ten minutes scouring the quieter alleys and I found my perfect establishment. Inside the small bar were just two people, a barman and a young woman sat at the bar. Neither seemed to be talking, they were definitely not laughing and Portishead played quietly on the stereo. The first icy mouthful tasted like gold as I waited for my change, thinking about which empty table I would take. The barman turned to hand me a few Baht and I could see my peaceful night crashing down as the woman also turned to me. I felt her eyes sizing me up and saw her mouth opening to form a word.

'Hi,' she said, leaving me lost for words. Since I'd left Koh Pha Ngan I had struggled to utter a social word to anyone. My days had been spent in sweet isolation, avoiding eye contact with everyone, but now this stranger had ruined everything.

'Hi,' I managed, glancing at my beer as I gave a weak smile and made a move towards a table.

'What are you doing tomorrow night?' she asked, her accent distinctly Irish. Now this had me stuck, my feet frozen to the spot as I desperately tried to think of a one word answer that would end our conversation and let me retreat, but regardless of the different replies swarming around my head, the word that escaped left me stunned and her smiling.

'Nothing,' I replied, puzzled by my response, as I continued my move towards the table once again. This time, step-by-step, the table was getting closer, the questions further away, but as I pulled a chair out, I glanced up to see her pulling one out too. She was joining me, uninvited, at my table of despair.

Sitting down, I watched as she did the same and for the first time I properly looked at her. She was dressed in a burgundy gypsy skirt, a dirty-white vest top and a burgundy bandana pulled over her short black hair. She wore no make-up and, although not distinctly ugly, she was all bones with hardly a trace of fat or muscle and had crooked teeth that stuck out with every smile. As I waited for her to speak and explain why she thought I might welcome her company, I glanced around for an escape route or an excuse to leave but she started speaking again before any plans could be formulated.

'Have you been snorkelling here yet?' she asked.

'No.'

'Well as you're not doing anything tomorrow night, do you want to come snorkelling?' she smiled.

'No,' I replied, hoping that if I could keep to one word answers she'd tire and go away.

'Why not?' she then asked, ruining my plan in an instant.

'I'm going home tomorrow morning,' I curtly replied.

'Oh, *oh*, I thought you said you were doing nothing. Oh, well if you're going home then too bad. How long have you been travelling for?' she chirpily continued. As I considered her answer, I realised that all in all, I'd been gone only a week. Not even a fortnight but *a week*. I couldn't tell her that, I couldn't admit to *a week*, not when I had been thinking this *year* would be the first of many.

'*Six months*,' I mumbled, feeling terrible for telling such a bad lie.

'Oh wow, I've only been away ten days. So where have you been?' she asked, but before I could begin making up places, she stood up and asked 'fancy another beer?'

An hour later and a couple more beers down, Rhoda, my Irish drinking buddy, knew everything about my action packed six months of travelling. How I'd briefly worked as a bar man in a bustling Sydney club, had bungee jumped in Cairns, seen crocodiles in Cape Tribulation, been offered a job on a cattle station, driven the Great Ocean Road, dived the Great Barrier Reef and learnt to surf in Byron Bay. The only thing I said I regretted from the whole journey was that I hadn't done a night snorkel with her, but time just wasn't on our side.

On the other hand, I learnt that Rhoda had gone to university only to fall out with her flat mates and decide that it wasn't quite as much fun as she'd hoped. Instead, she had spent the past few months scrimping and saving for a plane ticket. Travelling alone, she told me, had been tougher than expected. At first she felt too awkward to approach strangers but had realised that it was the only way she was going to be able to keep going. After all, she said, 'hiding away in a room, eating and drinking alone was beginning to drive her mad, distracting her from the surrounding beauty and freedom she'd left home for.' Listening to her, I couldn't help feel that I was giving up on backpacking too easily; maybe there wasn't an emergency at home, perhaps going back now would only shatter my dreams. After all, I was now being social again and it hadn't killed me. In fact, I was actually enjoying the conversation and the beers and hadn't noticed the bar filling up with other travellers, laughing and enjoying themselves, as I was now one of them.

As the beers kept coming and Rhoda and I continued talking, I learnt more about her home and her future plans and she in turn heard more lies about me. I figured that after the night was out we'd never see each other again, so I let slip that I was twenty, I played the guitar in a band back home and my sister had become my twin. For all I knew, she too was lying about wanting to work with a charity and settle down with a nice guy.

Soon the bar wasn't busy enough for us both, so we drank up and staggered to a club. The place we found felt like it should have been in the Caribbean, with palm thatched roof and walls and reggae music blasting out. The vibe inside was great, everyone was dancing and happy, us included. Several songs later, out on the dance floor, without warning, we had a moment. It lingered there for a second but that was enough time for her to lean in and kiss me. Then as quickly as it happened she pulled away, smiling. The next thing I knew, our dancing was getting closer and she was pressing her body against my own, before once again we were kissing. Shortly after, whilst surfacing for fresh air, we agreed to finish our beers and leave.

Opening my eyes the following morning, head spinning, I was relieved to find I was in my own bed, in my own little bungalow. That was comforting, but with the room spinning it was hard to remember what I'd done to get so hung-over. Looking down on the floor, I could hazily see an object that didn't belong there and closing one eye in an effort to focus my gaze, I realised I was looking at a blue condom, a used one. It was at that point that I suddenly became aware that I wasn't alone in the room. As memories of kissing Rhoda flooded back to me, I slowly turned to see if it was her or someone more attractive that I'd brought home.

Opening her eyes and smiling as I turned over, there was no mistaking it. I'd slept with Rhoda and as I lay there in a state of hung-over shock, she moved in closer and gave me a gentle kiss on the lips. This was all too much, my head was banging, the room spinning and I had Rhoda lying in my bed, kissing me. The only thing I could do was close my eyes and try to sleep off the nightmare.

Sleep must have come pretty easily as hours later I woke up, head still throbbing, but the room had stopped moving. Rhoda was still in the bed and asleep. Gently getting up so I wouldn't disturb her, I stepped onto the cold hard floor with my right foot and onto the cold rubbery condom with my left, causing me to use every bit of willpower not to jump and yell in disgust. Now I was up, I couldn't think what to do. I couldn't make a noise as the last thing I wanted was for her to wake up and start talking or asking me questions again. So putting on my board shorts, I headed for the door, the midday heat hitting me as I stepped out.

Outside, I decided to wander down to the beach and take a swim, hoping it would wake me up. On my previous swims in the bay I'd found the depth frustrating as it ranged from waist to shoulder deep, so I was never able to get out of my depth, no matter how far out I swam. Now though, feeling like I wouldn't have the strength to swim hard, it seemed ideal.

The tide was low and the warm water flat and glassy from the sun radiating its gleaming light across the gentle surface. After wading out for five minutes, the water had still only risen to the top of my shorts. Diving down and taking a handful of golden sand, I felt the warm water energising my weary body and mind. I remembered that I'd changed my mind about leaving and despite the bad start to the day, I couldn't help but feel I was making the right choice. I still needed to check my family were all alive and well but deep down I knew I'd overreacted, pointed out through my discussions with Rhoda. 'Shit,' I muttered under the water, remembering what else Rhoda and I had talked about. She thought I was leaving but I could easily fix that, say I was extending my flight by a few days. She also thought I was someone I wasn't and again I figured that too could be solved by never seeing her again. 'At least,' I reflected to myself, as I stood with my back to the land, 'she may not be my type but she's stopped me going home and it does leave only one more conquest with nearly three weeks left to go.'

Getting out of the water, mentally preparing myself for seeing her again, I briefly considered hiding behind a palm tree, spying on the bungalow and waiting until she'd left. But that was the child's way out and I felt I wanted to act like the twenty year old she thought I was. So I walked back in, and finding her still asleep, I pushed the door closed a little louder than necessary, watching her stir.

'Hi,' I said, taking a swig of the water bottle, feeling much better for the swim.

'Oh, hi. Have you been swimming?' she asked, rubbing sleep from her eyes and taking the water bottle from me.

'Yeah, thought it would help me get rid of my hangover. How are you feeling?'

'Like I need a swim too but I haven't got my bikini. Oh shit, aren't you meant to be leaving this morning? You haven't missed your boat have you?' she panicked.

'Er, yes and *no*. I've actually decided to stay a few more days and have changed my ticket,' I lied, immediately hoping she didn't question when I found time to do it.

'Oh cool, do you think you might be up for a night snorkel now then?' she asked, bringing us back to our first conversation.

'Not sure, why are you so keen on me snorkelling?'

'Well, they only operate with a minimum of two. Yesterday when I tried to book, they said I needed to find a friend, so... I found you,' she smiled. 'Come on, it's my last night on the island before I head back to smelly Bangkok and onto Brisbane, I know you've had a trip full of amazing experiences but this is my first one. Who knows, it might be as exciting as all your dives.'

'Okay, count me in,' I said, feeling guilty that I would be ruining her evening if I refused.

'Oh, that is sooo awesome. It's Matt, right?' she chuckled to herself, as she got up and disappeared into the bathroom, collecting her clothes off the floor as she went.

The day skipped by, nursing my hangover and reading through new guidebooks I'd decided to buy, this time on both Thailand and Australia. Rhoda hadn't stuck about, saying she'd book us both in for the snorkel and agreeing to meet me at the bar where we'd first met.

As the hours ticked by, I visited the internet café again, this time finding an email from my mum. All was well, everyone had survived the imaginary disaster in my mind, enjoying a weekend in London at my aunt's in the process. From there I wandered towards the bar, bumping into Rhoda en route. If our meeting felt awkward to her, she wasn't letting on. I wasn't sure whether I was now meant to kiss her, shake hands or nod but she seemed to have worked out exactly what was going on, giving me a wide smile and then bombarding me with questions about my afternoon, as we headed to the dive shop.

At the shop I was introduced to the dive master, a Kiwi called Andy. A short guy, built like a tank, with bleached blond locks, who was racing around the small shop getting equipment ready for the snorkel. As we took a seat and waited, another two women came in, greeting Andy, both excited by the night snorkel.

'*Oh great…* are there four of us?' I asked, feeling conned, as though I needn't have bothered coming along.

'Five, actually. There's another guy, due any minute now,' Andy pointed out, his energy making me feel lazy.

'Right, first things first,' Andy announced a couple of minutes later when our fifth member had arrived. 'Who hasn't snorkelled before?' he asked. As I looked around, I saw Rhoda put her hand up and I followed suit. 'Okay, two of you,' Andy said.

'But Matt has dived quite a bit, haven't you?' Rhoda said, referring to my make believe dives on the Great Barrier Reef.

'Ah... yeah. So I guess it's kinda the same, huh?' I said, trying to play it cool but inside kicking myself for having told her that.

'Yeah, more or less, mate. In fact this is quite a bit easier, less to remember and if you've dived the barrier reef, I'm sure you'll be fine,' he reassured me. 'Right, so... wetsuits. Matt, here you go, just put it on over your shorts mate,' he said, handing me a black suit, with stunted arms and legs. 'Ah, wrong way round Matt, not sure what they taught you in Oz but the zip should be at the back,' he then pointed out, as I had stepped in and was pulling it up. All eyes on me, I pushed it back down and turned it round, wishing I could just die.

Wetsuits on, Andy explained that he would be accompanying us on our swim, to lead us and hopefully keep us out of any trouble. He briefed us on the correct ways to use the equipment and showed us a dozen or so pictures of the sea life we would soon be seeing. Every image showed what could be easily mistaken for an alien; so brightly coloured and strange looking that they didn't belong to our world. It boggled my mind to think that we'd soon be swimming among such things, let alone seeing them, but I had to keep my thoughts to myself. In Rhoda's mind this was all old hat to me.

As we left the store, fins, torches, masks and snorkels in hand, I could feel the adrenaline start to pump its way through my veins, my nerves tingling with excitement. Walking along the road towards the harbour, we got strange looks from the masses of other backpackers who were all dressed up for the night and ready to head into the one of the many restaurants and bars. But as far I was concerned the curious onlookers were all missing out, just as I would have if Rhoda hadn't approached me.

A glimmering moon shimmered across the gentle waters around the long-tail boat that was going to take us out to the reef. Last to get in I pulled myself up and inside, finding a small bench to sit on right behind Rhoda. I wanted to talk to her, excited by what we were doing but I knew I'd slip up somewhere and show my ignorance that could untangle the web of lies I'd spun. So I sat in silence, taking in the experience and thinking how exciting it would be to properly dive and get right up close to the fish and coral as I had originally planned.

After about ten minutes of bouncing about as we travelled to the reef, the engine was cut and the only noise was the small wandering waves clunking against the hull and nearby cliffs. The lights of the island were still visible, but they were faint and looking down at the black abyss of water I began to get a little anxious about the thought of swimming about in it. Andy hadn't mentioned sharks or giant squids in his brief, but I was beginning to picture them down there, waiting for dinner.

Moments later, masks and fins on, it was the moment of truth. Rhoda went first, as I watched her disappear over the edge, her torch illuminating the inky water around her, shortly followed by the others. With only Andy, the Captain and I left in the boat, I tried to be a gentleman and offer Andy the next plunge but he insisted I go. So hands shaking, I closed my eyes and drew a deep breath, feeling the flippers pushing up as they hit the water. The snug wetsuit was immediately penetrated by the cold water, causing a chill to creep up my spine as I bobbed on the surface, looking around at the others.

Clenching my mouth around the snorkel, I faced my fears and stuck my face into the water. Away from the torch light the water looked as dark as the night sky. In the narrow beam of light an eerie underwater world, I had no idea existed, was illuminated. It sounded like Darth Vader was breathing in my ears as I floated around taking in the garden below.

As Andy gave us the signal to follow him on our intrepid journey along the reef, I ended up at the back of the pack, following five dancing beams as I slowly bobbed along. The first minute or two were spent swallowing mouthfuls of salty water as I tried to master the snorkel and balance my body at the same time, glad that Rhoda was too preoccupied to notice my rookie mistakes.

After another couple of minutes of floating about, I began to feel at one with my surroundings and started to relax and minimise my body movements. I could now hear the sound of water lapping around me and tiny eyes appeared out of the darkness, showing no signs of a body, just like a cartoon. Shoals of tiny fish froze momentarily in the torch beam, only to continue a few seconds later when they sensed the danger had gone.

At times it seemed we all swam too close together. In the first few minutes I collided with one or two of the others, their faces unrecognisable in masks of plastic and darkness.

It all felt like a game of follow the leader, without actually knowing who the leader was. Somehow it worked though, we all stuck together, or at least for a while but another collision made me slow down and purposely drift behind the group. Floating over a brightly decorated lobster, I had the urge to swim down and inspect its beauty close up. Letting the desire take control, I took out my snorkel and dived down, only to about five-feet but I immediately felt a sharp pain in my left ear stopping me from diving any further down.

Rising back up to the top, the pain in my ear subsided but I collided with one of the others again, or at least I thought I did. Swimming a little further along underwater I surfaced properly. Treading water, I looked around to make an apology for the collision, but found there was no torchlight and no one looking for an apology. Twenty-feet or so away, I could make out the flickers from five separate torches, which accounted for the other snorkelers. Realising I hadn't bumped into one of the others, I span around again searching for the thing that I'd hit, confronted only with darkness. I tried to imagine what I could have hit and all I could think about were sharks circling below. My isolated state away from the group would make me an easy target.

Taking in a mouthful of water as I splashed around, I desperately tried to see what was preying on me. I needed to get back to the boat but had no idea where it had gone. My only hope was to get back to the others and seek safety in numbers, hoping the sharks would pick off one of the others instead. Stroking and splashing my way towards them, with the torch light still on and swinging side to side over the surface, without warning my left hand connected with something solid. I knew it must be a shark and out of sheer terror, I let out a scream, not a girlie one, but a yell that told the world I was seriously screwed. Scrunching my face up in anticipation of the imminent attack, seconds went by and nothing. I could now see a torch beam making it's way over towards me and I started to calm down a little. I realised that my torch beam was settled on a plank of wood, the thing I'd just hit and maybe knocked when surfacing.

Feet away, I could now see Andy, bobbing in the water, also pointing his beam towards the driftwood.

'You okay, mate?' he asked.

'Yeah fine, I just got a little panicked when I bumped into this, that's all,' I replied, realising that an experienced diver like myself, shouldn't have been scared by a piece of wood.

'*Right*, well let's get back with the others,' he suggested, before adding, 'and stop waving your torch around so much, the light really pisses off the fish.'

For the rest of the swim I stayed on the surface and kept in close to the others, even overtaking one of them in an effort to avoid being left behind again. The further we went, the more I relaxed and the better the underwater display became, as both the coral types and colours rapidly changed with every few metres and as my eyes adjusted to the conditions more tiny fish became visible.

At the end of the snorkel I was disappointed to see the boat again, hoping it might have lost us for a while, leaving us more time to explore the dark waters. Before climbing out of the water, Andy suggested we should turn off our lights for a moment. Following his instruction, we floated about in the darkness for a minute, until much to our surprise the water around us began to glow. It was an incredible experience. Lifting my hand out of the water it had an eerie luminosity to it, which I could see was also enchanting the others.

When a few minutes later Andy announced it was time to head back, I felt far from ready to hit terra firma so soon. It was as if I'd been given a free taste of a highly addictive drug and as the boat bounced across the water towards the land, all I could think about was how much more there was down there to see and explore.

Leaving the dive shop a little while later, feeling energised from the experience, Rhoda and I headed out to dinner. I could sense it wasn't going to be a repeat of the previous evening though; she kept off the beer, opting for water and although friendly enough she made no attempts to be tactile or make mention of the previous night. In my mind I wasn't sure if it was because she was waiting for me to make the first move, which in all honesty I didn't want to do, or if she genuinely didn't want to repeat last night. Which since I couldn't remember how I'd performed, I found a little disconcerting, in case I'd put her off.

As we finished the meal and sat chatting, she told me she needed an early night to pack and be fresh for an early start, which signalled that she wanted to go back alone. However, I'd decided through dinner that although I didn't really want sex with her again, if she felt the same because of a poor drunken performance then I wanted another shot, just to show her I was better when sober. There seemed no easy way to approach the situation and as we got up to say goodbye, I saw that my best way in was to get a snog. As she went for a friendly kiss on the cheek, I slyly moved across aiming for her lips but she wasn't having any of it.

'Oh…no,' she blurted, looking embarrassed for the fist time, 'I'm sorry Matt but I can't.'

'Why not?' I quizzed. 'Did I do something wrong last night?'

'Oh, no… *no*. Well, not that I remember anyway. Look Matt, I didn't mean to… I mean last night wasn't what I had intended. You're a nice guy,' as she spoke, I could feel a familiar rejection coming on, she called me *nice*, 'and I'm off to Australia, you're heading home, we'll never see each other again. I didn't want a one night stand and certainly not a second one, besides you're not really my type. I'm sorry,' she said, this time kissing me on the cheek and walking away.

Left stranded outside the restaurant, trying to work out exactly what had happened, but sensing it was definitely for the best, I felt a gentle tap on the back of my shoulder. Slowly, I turned around expecting to see Rhoda again, having changed her mind. However, the woman staring back at me wasn't Rhoda.

'*Lola*? What the hell are you doing here?' I said, moving in towards her for a hug. She looked so healthy, her hair was still dreadlocked and her skin had a deep olive tan.

'What do you mean what am *I* doing here? What are *you* doing here? I thought you'd have been and gone through Thailand weeks ago,' she quizzed.

'Well that was the plan but then I thought you'd be in New Zealand right about now,' I stated.

'Huh, funny, it seems plans changed for both of us, but hey we're both here, how amazing!' Lola exclaimed. '*So*, Matt what are you doing right now?'

'I was just going to head back to my room and sleep.'

'Oh that's boring - it's early. I was about to meet a friend for a beer, if you fancy joining us?' she asked, still noticeably excited at our meeting.

'Yeah sure, why not?' I said, as we headed into a small bar next door.

'So what ever happened to that email you were meant to send me, telling me your plans and dates?' she asked, as we ordered.

'Well, I somehow managed to leave your address behind at home in my guidebook. I kept meaning to ask my mum to find it and tell me the address but haven't really had a good chance yet. Besides, I didn't really think you'd still be Thailand,' I said, knocking my beer against hers, 'cheers.'

'I didn't think I'd still be here either, but my plans have changed a little as you can see,' she replied, looking over my shoulder and smiling at someone behind me. 'Hi Noodle,' she said, as a man came round to kiss her on the cheek. '*Noodle*?' I blurted out, a little louder than I'd intended, wondering how many people have that nickname. As I spoke, his attention shifted away from Lola and onto myself. The man before me was wearing a faded, old, flowery shirt and a pair of baggy green shorts down to just below his knees. His hair was shaved off to stubble but I could see a receding line peering through. Stepping forwards, he thrust out his right hand for me to shake and in an instant I could see from his eyes that it was the same Noodle from Newquay.

'Noodle,' he said with a firm shake.

'Matt,' I replied, wondering if he might recognise me too.

After a surreal minute spent standing around making small talk, I didn't know whether I was more surprised by the fact that Lola was still in Thailand, or that she knew Noodle. Finding a table directly underneath a rather wobbly ceiling fan, the three of us sat down. My eyes moved back and forth between Lola and Noodle. Although it had been less than a year and a half since I'd met Noodle in Newquay, I

70

couldn't help but think he looked much older, as though he'd aged ten years.

As Lola began to explain the history of our relationship to Noodle, I was dying to ask them both endless questions and seeing a break in conversation, I jumped right in.

'Noodle, you haven't ever lived in Newquay before have you?' I asked, not wanting to beat around the bush.

'I did, yeah mate, how did you know that?' he replied, his smile fading from his face as he looked a little stunned.

'I think I might have met you down there, the summer before last, when I stayed for a weekend.'

'You could well have done, that was the last summer I spent there, although I'm sorry I can't picture you, are you a surfer?' he asked.

'No, not yet, but I want to learn. I'm going to give it a go when I get to Australia,' I replied, wishing again that I'd it tried back in Newquay.

'Well, Australia's a good place to learn,' he commented, although without a trace of enthusiasm.

'First though, I want to learn to dive here,' I said, as thoughts of the snorkel rushed back.

'Oh yeah?' Noodle asked, again lacking lustre. I couldn't help but wonder if my presence was bothering him.

'Matt, I don't think you can dive can you?' Lola said, saving Noodle from further conversation.

'Well no, not yet, but I want to learn,' I replied, a little puzzled as to how she would know I couldn't, or if somehow she knew of my lies to Rhoda.

'That's not what I mean. Back when we were kids, I remember you burst an eardrum diving into a swimming pool. It was you wasn't it?' she asked.

'What? Back when I was nine? Well, yeah I did, but what's that got to do with me diving now? My ear's fine now,' I answered, remembering the acute pain I felt when I'd tried to swim down on the snorkel.

'So, can you equalize the ear now?' she asked, her question making no sense to me.

'Can I what? ...Equalize?' I asked, as I watched Lola demonstrate what she meant. It was the same thing that the old guy from my flight had shown me to reduce the popping sensation from my ears and it was then that I realised why I hadn't been able to relieve the pressure in my left ear to the same extent as the right. The left drum had been burst in a freak accident, leaving me in pain for weeks and with

71

slightly reduced hearing. Now, years later, it was coming back to haunt me.

'No, I don't think I can, you're right. How do you still remember that?' I gloomily asked, watching as Noodle got up and went to the bar for another drink, my own beer hardly touched.

'I'm working at a dive shop here, everyday I have to check people can do it, warning them of the risks and each time I remember back to seeing you writhing in pain at the edge of the pool,' she explained. '*Oh and don't mind Noodle, he's okay once he knows you but not very good with strangers*,' she whispered.

As I sat quietly, taking in everything Lola had just told me about my ear and never being able to dive, the thing that stuck in my mind was what she'd said about Noodle. It made me question if it was really the same guy I had met, who had saved the weekend of two teenagers he didn't know, all by being friendly and introducing them into his world.

As Noodle returned to the table and sat down, I tried to think of what I could say that would open him up, as he focused on peeling the label off his beer bottle and silently listening to Lola and I talk.

'Would my ear affect me if I wanted to surf as well?' I asked him, hoping that a surfing question might interest him, although I realised a 'yes' would have been devastating, ruling out both of my planned water activities in one swift blow.

'I wouldn't have thought so,' he said, 'depends on how bad it is. Can you swim underwater alright?' he asked, as again I thought back to the pain during the snorkel.

'Most of the time it's fine, I only get pain if I go too deep,' I answered, deciding that the truth was better than lying.

'Well, I wouldn't worry then, unless of course you're planning on surfing fifty foot waves,' he joked, smiling for the first time that evening.

After that Noodle fell silent again, and as I could feel fatigue taking a grip, I decided to leave Lola and Noodle alone, agreeing to meet up with her the following evening for dinner. On my way back, I remembered that the Noodle of Newquay only travelled where the waves were breaking and realised that maybe that was the problem, there were no waves in Koh Phi Phi and without them, he'd lost his shine.

It was nearly midday when I woke up, the rain hammering against the windows. Rubbing the sleep from my eyes and staring outside, I could see the wind was howling, battering the nearby palm trees and giant puddles had begun to form on the surrounding lawn.

It was hardly weather for going out, but it did seem right for a swim as I would be getting wet anyway. Putting on my red boardshorts, I opened the door, immediately feeling the strength of the wind as it tried to rip the handle out of my hand. Splashing through the puddles, the rain was stinging, driven into my bare flesh by the gales. Down on the beach it was even worse, the sand was being whipped up and was joining forces with the water, to really hurt.

As I stood on the edge of the beach looking out into the water, there was nobody around, no one in the sea. Normally there would be dozens, but they were obviously more sensible, hiding away in their rooms until the storm passed. As I quickly debated the sanity of going into the sea in such a storm, a thud shook the ground to my right. A huge coconut had fallen from the tree towering thirty-feet above me and looking around, I could see it wasn't the first. Along the beach they were dropping like lethal bombs. Realising I had to move, the safest place now seemed to be the choppy water where could I see anything coming.

Already soaked from the downpour as I waded in, the water felt a degree or two warmer than the blinding rain and diving under the shallow surface the howling and stinging suddenly ended. Just inches below the turbulent top I was enveloped in a world of peace and serenity, the warmth of the water enticing me to stay under. As my lungs cried out for oxygen I quickly broke the surface, back into hell, before diving back down and skimming the seabed now a couple of feet under. I followed this pattern as I headed further out into the bay, enjoying the paradoxical world.

After ten minutes of rising and diving, I stopped and stood up. The water was just below my shoulders, but with the occasional small wave coming through and lifting me off my feet, before planting me back down a few feet further back in. The back of my head was now facing the fierce wind and, rubbing the salt water out of my eyes, I could now see the majesty of the bay and the sheets of rain as they shot across the water. For a moment, I thought I saw something else breaking the surface close to the deserted shore but, as I focused on that spot for a few more seconds, there was nothing.

Back under the water, in the warmth, I began swimming back towards the shore although I was keen to keep swimming for as long as I could, or until the storm passed, whichever came first. Under the water, I kept a look out for fish and crabs but there was nothing, no sign of life. Back on the surface the wind felt like it was getting stronger and the sea more choppy. Suddenly, ten-feet away the surface of the water broke and a man surfaced, before ducking straight down under again.

In the brief moment he'd risen for air I wasn't sure if he'd seen me and as I stood my ground, I tried to make out where he'd gone but the surface of the water was simply too turbulent. As I too went below the surface, looking out for him, I felt robbed. I thought the bay was all mine and the experience mine alone, but for all I knew there were countless others like me enjoying the worlds of calm and chaos.

As I rose again, this time I could see him. He had chosen to stand up in what was now waist high water, facing into the driving rain, eyes wide, staring at me. The first thing I noticed was a series of scars running across his chest and left shoulder. Moving my eyes higher, I realised I knew the stranger.

'Noodle!' I shouted, moving in closer. Breaking his trance as I spoke, he finally looked at me.

'*Matt*? What the hell are you doing here?' he shouted.

'Enjoying the storm, same as you I guess!' I replied, and without warning he dived under the surface and vanished. I stood for a minute scanning the water, waiting for him to surface but there was no sign of him, he was gone.

I kept swimming for another few minutes, but the novelty had been lost. I was no longer alone and having to constantly move in and out of the water was beginning to exhaust me. Back on the beach, the wind seemed to be finally easing off, but now out of the water I felt frozen, wanting to stay and watch the sea, even bump into Noodle again, but I needed to dry off and warm up.

The afternoon passed quickly. Shortly after I'd dried off, the rain and wind eased away and the sun broke through the clouds. By mid-afternoon only a few scattered puddles around the roads remained as evidence that it had rained. When I met up with Lola later that evening I wasn't expecting to see Noodle but he was there and immediately I wished he wasn't. I didn't want a repeat of the uncomfortable drinks from the night before, but this evening he seemed a little different.

74

'Hi Matt,' he said, 'some storm huh?' he smiled, as we made our way to a restaurant.

'Some fucking storm alright,' Lola butted in, 'I was stuck out on a boat. We were just getting ready when it blew in. Wouldn't have been so bad if we were under the water already but dealing with five first-time divers on a stormy sea just wasn't fun, especially when two of them got seasick.'

'It was better in the bay then, I guess,' I offered.

'Yeah, Noodle said he bumped into you there. You're both mad swimming in that. I hope you weren't stupid enough to follow Noodle out, Matt,' she said.

'Out?'

'I swam out of the bay into the open sea Matt,' Noodle explained, 'don't worry he didn't follow me,' he reassured her.

'You went out of the bay? Why?' I asked.

'Noodle thinks anything safe is too boring, don't you?' Lola replied, noticeably unimpressed.

'It's not that Lola, it's just that the bay is too shallow, I wanted something a little more fun and challenging.'

'So, you swam out into the open water during the storm?' I asked.

'I just swam up to the next beach, I don't see what the big deal is,' Noodle replied, becoming a little defensive.

'Yeah, well, it's fucking irresponsible Noodle,' Lola said, 'you know what? I'm not hungry. Matt, let's do dinner tomorrow night. Noodle, fucking grow up,' she said before turning around and storming off.

This left me in an awkward place, standing next to Noodle, unsure what had gotten Lola so riled but feeling I had witnessed something I shouldn't have done. Just as I was about to make an excuse to save Noodle doing it, he turned and said 'You fancy pizza?' his eyes burning with anger.

'Yeah, okay,' I replied, feeling completely unsettled and a little too scared to say no, as we headed into a pizza restaurant nearby.

As we sat down and ordered beers, I sensed that his mind was on the row with Lola but if we were dining together there were some questions I wanted answers to.

'So are you still surfing?' I asked, watching him pull a tobacco pouch out of his pocket.

'Well, right now I'm on a little break. Things got pretty hairy for me a few months back. I had a bad session and ended up slicing my shoulder and chest to shreds,' he said, glancing up from the cigarette he was rolling.

'Yeah, I noticed your scars in the water earlier, what happened?'

'I was surfing in Indo and hit a reef,' he said.

'Indo?'

'Indonesia,' he clarified, before continuing, 'I went there on a bit of suicide mission after I lost my girlfriend in an accident.'

As he spoke I felt a chill run up my spine, my mind reeling back to the beauty he was with in Newquay.

'That's terrible. Was she in Newquay with you that summer I met you?' I asked, hoping it wasn't who I was thinking of.

'Fran? Yeah, she probably was.' He nodded, downing the rest of his beer and signalling at a waitress for another.

The conversation fell silent between us again as we waited for the meal, both of us, I imagined, reflecting on Fran, who I'd instantly fallen for during the beach party as I glimpsed her across the fire.

'So, your friend Lola's pretty fiery,' Noodle said, finally speaking again, as he began rolling another cigarette.

'She seems to be, although I only knew her as a child, so I can't really remember seeing that side of her before.'

'She pulled me back from the brink you know?' he remarked.

'What do you mean?'

'When she and I met, it was not too long after I'd got the scars. I'd left Indo and found my way to Vietnam where I was trying to get the pieces of my life back together only to end up a bit of a recluse, angry at everything. I was desperate to move on but without an idea of where I could go that would be any better,' he said.

'So, are you and Lola… you know? …an item?' I asked.

'No… it's complicated,' he said, before adding, 'she's a rare soul,' changing the conversation to ask me about my travels so far.

Over more beers I told Noodle about the bet I'd made with Ben and Kermit, feeling that as a guy he might understand and appreciate it.

'So you've managed two so far, that's not bad going,' Noodle smiled 'And you've got pictures for the guys?'

'Well, no, so far I've got none in that respect. Truth be told though, I'm more concerned with trying to keep backpacking for the month than pulling, it's just kind of happened so far,' I replied truthfully.

'Well, you've got just over another couple of weeks,' Noodle said, holding his beer up and grinning.

'Yeah, well who knows, maybe at Christmas when I'm on Bondi Beach it'll happen,' I said, flashing a confident yet hollow smile, as I really did feel over the whole thing.

'You're spending Christmas on Bondi?' Noodle asked.

'Yeah and New Year in Sydney too. I've seen pictures of the fireworks over the Opera House, it all looks pretty spectacular,' I replied. 'What about you?'

'Er, not really sure at the moment, may just end up here. As I said before I'm really feeling quite stuck,' he replied. 'Anyhow, mate, I'm going to have to call it a night, I'm knackered,' Noodle said, as he abruptly got up and left, looking like he suddenly had somewhere to go.

The following morning, I headed straight to Lola's dive shop hoping to catch her before she went out on a boat. Walking in, I could see she was busy talking to a couple, booking them onto a dive. So, hovering about waiting, I picked up a book on marine life and began flicking through the pages, fascinated by the colourful fish, I'd never get to see up close.

'Morning Matt,' Lola said, coming over and giving me a hug as the couple left, 'I'm really sorry to have left you with Noodle last night but his flippant attitude really pisses me off at times.'

'It was alright actually, we talked, he told me what happened to him, how his girlfriend had died. I can kind of see why he is as he is,' I said, hoping she understood what I meant.

'I know, he came over to mine last night and we had a long chat ourselves,' she said, looking like she was about to say more but stopped.

'Oh, *right*. Well, I just wanted to check that you're okay. Same time for dinner tonight?' I asked as I headed back out of the shop, wishing I could have been like the couple before me, signing up for a dive.

That evening it was clear that Noodle had also caught up with Lola and sweetened things, as the air between them seemed fine. I was finding it great to have friends to share my evenings with, knowing that I wouldn't slip back into the lonely state I was in when I arrived on the island and now sensing that Noodle also needed the company.

'So, Matt, Noodle told me you're going to spend Christmas on Bondi Beach, *why*?' Lola asked me.

'That's my plan and well it's *Bondi*, it's kind of the thing to do,' I replied.

'Well, I guess but I wouldn't have thought of you as a Bondi kind of guy, especially as you said you hated the full moon party,' she said.

'What do you mean? It's just a massive barbie on the beach isn't it?'

'Well, not really. It's a huge beach party with thousands of people crammed in...' she paused, 'why don't you come up to Byron?'

'What Byron Bay?' I asked.

'Yeah, and she's got a good point mate, Byron will definitely be better that Sydney, especially if you're wanting to try surfing. In Byron you could try surfing on Christmas Day, now that would be pretty special, you'll never manage that on Bondi, I assure you' Noodle added, as he tried to relight the cigarette he was smoking.

'Surely Byron Bay will be just as hectic though?' I asked, although I had no idea.

'It'll be busy, sure, but then everywhere's busy at Christmas and New Year. I think that you'll enjoy Byron better than Bondi, besides we'll be there.' Lola said, smiling.

'You're going to Byron for Christmas?' I asked, recalling Noodle telling me the night before that he'd probably just stick around.

'Well, yeah. Noodle and I had a bit of a chat late last night and we decided to head on to Oz for Christmas and New Year, then we're going to fly down to New Zealand and continue my original trip, together,' she smiled. Although, I was a little confused at what I was hearing.

'I think I need to just get away from here,' Noodle explained, looking a little awkward, 'I've got a surfboard back in Byron at a mate's place. It's been too long since I've surfed and I've heard New Zealand's got more than just sheep, so I figured I'd give it a go,' he added as he ran a hand over his balding scalp and smiled at Lola.

Listening to Noodle talk, he was like a different person to the one I'd so far encountered in Koh Phi Phi, closer to the Noodle I remembered in Newquay. Continuing to talk about Christmas in Byron Bay, I heard that Noodle had already booked them seats on a flight from the nearby town of Krabi down to the Gold Coast, which meant they were getting from point to point with minimum fuss and travel. I, on the other hand, had been planning to spend Christmas in Sydney, in part because I was getting into Sydney on the twenty-third. Now that Lola and Noodle had presented the option of Byron Bay, I knew that I would need to catch a bus or a train up the four hundred plus miles between the two places on the day I arrived in Australia or worse - on Christmas Eve.

The days that followed flew by in a blur. Lola managed to get me two free afternoon snorkels through her dive shop, and on the other days Noodle and I hung out drinking beer and playing cards. As we sat around enjoying a life of leisure, Noodle was getting increasingly animated, especially when we talked about surfing, which he seemed to be missing more than he'd realised.

When the time came to leave the island and head back to Bangkok alone, I was itching to get to Australia. As good as the past few days in Thailand had been, they had been spent talking and thinking about the next stage of my adventure in so much detail that I really just wanted to get there and experience it. Saying my goodbyes to Lola and Noodle over beers the night before, I was secretly glad they weren't joining me on my journey to Byron Bay. Although I would have welcomed their experience and company, I felt it was something I needed to do alone, just to eradicate the little bit of lingering doubt that I was capable of independent travel.

Six

Lady luck had failed to shine on me during the flight to Sydney as it had to Bangkok, surrounding me with middle-aged couples, although at least this time my television worked. As we touched down and trundled along Sydney runway towards our parking space, the pilot announced the local time as six o'clock in the morning. Converted into Thai time, which my body was still operating on, it was two o'clock in the morning. At least with a twelve-hour bus ride up to Byron Bay, which I was still to endure before the day was out, I knew I could catch up on some sleep en route.

Passport in hand, I picked up my backpack from the luggage carousel and headed for the green *Nothing to Declare* exit. Just about to make my way through, a friendly looking female customs officer stopped me in my tracks and asked me to follow her. For an unknown reason I began to think I'd been mistaken for a celebrity or VIP and that she was going to offer me red carpet entry into her country, after all I really couldn't see any other reason for the detour. My illusion was instantly shattered when she left me with a less friendly looking middle-aged man. He was about six-inches shorter than myself, with a pencil thin moustache and greasy slicked back receding hair. As he muttered something about putting my bag down on the spotless steel desk before me, I almost cracked up with laughter at his whiney Australian accent that seemed so different to the nicer lady who'd led me to his desk. Repressing a piss-taking smile that was fighting to surface, I watched as he proceeded to open up my large backpack. Striking fool's gold almost immediately the officer found my dirty, smelly laundry, but it didn't seem to sway his latex covered hands from sifting through it all.

Stopping momentarily from his search to look me in the eyes, the officer's questioning began.

'So you've just come from Thailand, *yes*?' he asked.

'Yeah,' I replied, weary eyed and looking around for a seat to relax on whilst he wasted both our time.

'Did you try the opium while you were there?' he casually asked, causing alarm bells to ring in my head, instantly snapping me out of my relaxed state of jet lag. Looking him straight in the eye, with seriousness, my mind briefly flashed back to Claire locked up in a

Thai prison, as I said, '*No*, I don't do drugs.' Seemingly registering my comment, he nodded and continued to pick his way through my bag.

'Did you try the magic mushroom shakes over there?' he stopped to ask, moments later.

'No, *I - don't - do – drugs,*' I slowly repeated, thinking maybe I'd not been clear enough before, hoping he'd quickly realise he was sniffing up the wrong tree with me.

'Did you go to the full moon party on Koh Phan Ngan?' he asked, his trimmed brows frowning.

'I did, but I didn't take any drugs there either,' I replied, predicting where his questioning was about to lead to.

'*What* not even any ecstasy? Diet pills? Marijuana?' I could sense he was clutching at straws but I wasn't about to take his bait, especially as I was completely innocent.

'Look, I don't even smoke cigarettes. I drink beer, yes, I drink coffee with a bit of sugar, I admit those, but that's all, I don't touch anything else,' I pleaded, exhausted by his questioning and watching him nod again before opening up my guidebook and flicking through the pages, stopping to read any notes that had been scribbled in the margins.

As I watched his every move, I felt my hopes of a year in Australia were suddenly in jeopardy. The snide officer seemed to be looking for the slightest reason to put me back on a plane. Picking up a red lighter, that I'd forgotten was still in my bag, he glanced up, reading my tired expressions before he spoke.

'I thought you said you don't smoke,' he stated, holding it up and grinning.

'*I don't,*' I replied, stifling a bored yawn.

'Then why do you have a cigarette lighter? Surely if you don't smoke either dope or cigarettes you don't need a lighter?' he sneered.

'I *don't* smoke but I used it for lighting mosquito coils every night,' I replied.

'You know these are prohibited on aeroplanes?' he asked, deciding that if he couldn't harass me for my non-existent drug habits then he'd try another tack.

'*Are they*? Sorry, I wasn't aware. It was only the second time I've flown,' I replied, glancing over my shoulder, hoping that the nice lady was going to come back and lead me through the VIP exit she was meant to.

'That's no excuse. Can I see your wallet please?' he asked, as I handed it over.

Picking his way through my wallet, he produced a small swab and wiped it through the different compartments before handing the swab to a nearby colleague, who then walked away with it.

'What's that all about?' I asked.

'It'll tell us if you've had any drugs in your wallet before... Does this concern you?' he asked, staring straight in my eyes.

'*No*, I can't say it does,' I wearily replied. 'Largely because I've never actually done any drugs. *Although,* I did once hear that about ninety nine percent of all bank notes contain drug traces, so having had money in my wallet in the past it wouldn't come as a complete shock,' as soon the last words left my mouth I realised that I shouldn't have said them, knowing that stooping to his level wouldn't help, not when the cards were stacked in his favour.

Minutes of silence passed as the officer began to repack my bag, ramming things back in with indifference before his colleague returned and informed us that the test was clear.

'Are you surprised by this, given your theory of banknotes?' my officer asked. Looking down into his eyes I searched for some humour in his face but it was set in stone. I wanted to say *Well, yes I am actually, because I was cutting coke last night with that very credit card you swabbed and you blatantly missed the three kilos of heroin in the bottom of my bag, not to mention the condom filled with pills that's stuffed rather uncomfortably up my arse.* But for fear of being believed, strip-searched and thrown on the first plane back home, I just muttered a weary, '*no...* can I go now?'

With great reluctance on behalf of the Australian government, my wish was granted. Stepping out into the arrivals area, the automatic doors closed firmly behind me, while in front a congregation of strangers stood around waiting for a familiar face to emerge. Walking past them, I couldn't help smiling at the thought that I was now officially in Australia, home for the next year, and knowing that within hours I'd be in Byron Bay, smoking a spliff on the beach.

'The last available bus to Byron Bay left about fifteen minutes ago,' the chubby woman at the airport travel counter blandly told me.

'Shit,' I whispered, thinking of the time wasted by the customs official, 'when's the next available one?'

'The twenty-seventh from Sydney bus station,' she said.

'No, I mean today,' I replied, hoping she'd misunderstood me.

'*I know*, but the next available bus or train up to Byron Bay is on the twenty-seventh. Tomorrow is Christmas Eve, you know?' she said, as though I was an idiot for asking.

'So, hang on, let me get this straight, you're telling me that all the buses and trains are all completely full and there's no other way of getting to Byron Bay until the twenty-seventh?' I loudly questioned, beginning to wonder if all Australians were as frustrating to deal with as my last two encounters. 'How else am I going to get there?' I asked, glancing over my shoulder at the long impatient queue waiting behind me.

'You could hire a car and drive,' she impatiently said.

'I don't have a licence,' I moaned, thinking for a moment that I should have bought one on Khao San Road.

'Or fly,' she said.

'Okay, yeah. When's the next available flight?' I asked, knowing it would be the least cost effective way, but realising I was out of options.

'The next available flight to the Gold Coast or Brisbane is on the twenty-seventh as well. Would you like to book your seat for a bus or flight on the twenty-seventh?' she asked.

'No,' I muttered, as I dejectedly walked away, desperately trying to think of other ways to get there.

Moving away from the travel desk, I found a bench and sat down, sending a quick text to Lola to explain my problem. Seconds went by, which then stretched into minutes, as I stared at the phone willing it to into life to give me a solution. Nothing came.

Wasting time by being frustrated and depressed wasn't getting me any closer to Byron Bay nor helping with my fatigue. So, pulling myself up from the floor and shouldering my backpack, I headed out towards the bus terminal for a journey into the city to find the hostel that Noodle had recommended, should I need it. On the same piece of paper was the name of his friend's hostel in Byron Bay, aptly named *Liquid Dreams Backpackers*, although studying the words as I waited for the bus, there seemed no way I was going to make it there before Christmas.

Strange faces gave me even stranger looks as I walked into the Sydney hostel. The girl behind the counter, a backpacker herself, glanced up from the book she was reading, shook her head and said, 'sorry mate, *full…*' before turning her attention back to her book.

'What can I do then? Is there another hostel nearby?' I asked not wanting to emulate my first morning in Bangkok.

'You could try *One World* just round the corner,' she replied, jabbing a finger to the left without bothering to look up.

'Okay, *thanks for all your help*,' I sarcastically replied as I left.

Around the corner turned out to be a solid ten-minute walk uphill, in the heavy rain. Finally reaching *One World Backpackers*, I peered in through the cracked windowpane, and pulled open the heavy door, ready for more bad news. However, I found luck, when the balding middle-aged owner, with a gruff voice, led me down a musty smelling corridor towards the last vacant bed in the building. The room was deserted, but around the dozen or so bunk beds the floor was littered with their clothes and belongings and the unpleasant damp smell from the corridor had significantly increased. As bad as it was I really didn't have the energy, nor the resolve, to trudge about the city in search of something better, so I admitted defeat and threw my bag down on the nearest piece of empty carpet.

'So how many nights?' The owner asked, putting a hand across his greasy scalp.

'I'm not sure; I'm trying to find a way to reach Byron Bay before Christmas. How much is it a night?'

'Thirty-two bucks mate, you say Byron huh?'

'*Thirty-two dollars*? Per night? Really?' The price was an incredible increase on the dirt cheap en suite private rooms of Thailand.

'Yeah, you said you're wanting to go to Byron mate?'

'I did, but it seems there's no way of getting there before Christmas,' I said, pulling out my wallet and counting a hundred dollars out in the odd plastic bank notes, figuring I'd be stuck for at least three nights.

'Well, you should ask the two Canadian boys about it, they're headed that way tomorrow and were wanting some people to share the petrol with,' he suggested as he reached out for my money.

'Tomorrow? Canadians? Are they around, have you seen them today?'

'Oh yeah mate, Ryan and whatever the other one's called, they're upstairs getting a head start on the grog.'

'*The grog*?'

'Yeah mate, they're getting blotted, full as a boot, ya know?' he clarified, seemingly enjoying my confusion.

'*You mean they're getting drunk*?' I asked, hoping I'd deciphered his words correctly, before glancing up at the wall clock behind the owner. 'It's *only* ten-thirty in the morning here, right?'

'That's right mate, now are you only gonna stay one night then or what?' he asked, thumbing the money I'd given him.

Walking into the communal lounge I felt like the school kid with no friends, timidly approaching a table full of the cool boys, hoping for acceptance. The owner had told me that the guys I was looking for both had brown curly hair and could have been mistaken for brothers and probably, he thought, the only ones drinking beer. The lounge was bustling with a dozen or so people crowded around a loud blurry television in the corner. Others sat around talking and eating breakfast, but I couldn't see anyone fitting the description of the beer drinking Canadians. I was about to walk out and look for another lounge, thinking I'd gone to the wrong place, when heading back towards the door I heard an eruption of laughter coming from beyond the wall, the sound making its way through a nearby window. Looking out, I could see a patio area partially under the cover of a tarpaulin, from where the steady rain dripped off the end and onto a vacant table. To the right of the window was a table where three lads sat around drinking beer, two of them with curly hair. '*Bingo*,' I muttered to myself, looking around for a way out onto the patio.

The table was already littered with empty beer bottles and an ashtray full of cigarette butts, which wouldn't have looked out of place if not for the box of Coco Pops beside them. Not one of them noticed me walking over through the rain, their attention focused on a game of cards.

'Er... is one of you Ryan?' I asked, huddled under the end of the tarpaulin and looking at one of the two with curly hair.

All three card players fell silent as they turned to stare at me. The scruffiest looking of the trio, long curly hair, messily sticking out as though he'd just woken up, a thin beard, and ripped t-shirt, held my gaze with a huge but confused grin, whilst the other two turned back to their cards.

'Hey buddy, yeah, I'm Ryan, what's up?' the scruffy one replied, his accent was definitely a North American one, making him my man.

'The old guy at reception said you might have a space in your car going to Byron Bay tomorrow?' I asked, flinching as a drop of water fell down my back. Ryan gestured for me to pull up another chair and join their table.

'Hhhmmm... I just promised the back seats to a couple not more than fifteen minutes ago, although... I guess if you don't mind being squashed up for the whole journey, then we could fit you in. You don't have a lot of luggage or a surfboard do you?' Ryan asked, as the other Canadian glanced up and gave me a smile and a nod.

'No, just a backpack,' I smiled, feeling like I wanted to yell out in celebration.

Within seconds, the deal was done; I was presented with a complementary ice cold beer and a hand of cards before being duly introduced to the others. The other Canadian, Scott, looked like he was off to a country club, with a smart polo shirt and tailored shorts, but the old man had been right, he did look a lot like Ryan, except without the beard and slightly shorter smarter hair. The other guy at the table was a thin German called Mirco, with short spiky blond hair and who, judging by his bleary eyes, seemed to be struggling with a hangover, but beer in hand was determined to beat it. Unlike the Canadians who'd been in Australia for over six months, Mirco had only arrived a fortnight before and had landed a job in a local hotel as a chef.

Over cards and beer, I told the boys about my travels to date, going into details about Claire, Rhoda, Noodle and Lola. Ryan in particular became quite keen to meet Claire and Lola, after I'd offered a brief description of them both, and all three seemed to have met a Rhoda in their time.

Hours whirled past in a beer soaked blur, with round-after-round of *shithead*, the card game that kept us amused for hours on end. Due to the early start we'd made, pacing was essential, as was eating, so as the sun began to set behind the wall of our city hostel, we decided to move our drinking to the nearby pub, with the added intention of grabbing some pub food to save any sloppy attempts at cooking in the crowded communal kitchen.

On my way back from a trip to the bar, hands full with the smaller Australian equivalent of a pint, strangely called a schooner, I was disappointed to discover I'd just missed meeting the couple I'd be sharing the back seat with up to Byron Bay.

'I hope for your sake your sitting next to her and not the boyfriend, buddy, he seems like a real grumpy bastard,' Ryan slurred.

'Yeah, well, I'm not going to try it on with any girl with a boyfriend. Not anymore…' I reflected. '*Where's my beer gone?*' I asked, before Scott handed me one of the two fresh schooners I'd put down next to him only moments before. It was then that I realised just how drunk I was, although it was the ten minutes of throwing up in the toilet shortly after that confirmed my suspicion.

86

Stumbling home, with the occasional wall or lamppost for support, Ryan reminded me that we were due to hit the roads in less than four hours at the ungodly hour of five a.m.. Creeping into my dorm room, nothing much registered beside the fact that I couldn't remember which bed was mine. I didn't want to put the light on and wake everybody else up, so I used the dim light of my phone trying desperately to locate my bag, which I was sure I'd left next to my bed. Squinting in the darkness, I tripped up on a discarded pair of shoes and fortunately fell into my unopened bag, noticing for the first time a loud croaky snore emanating from a higher bed. My bag was between two empty beds, neither of which looked slept in, so I took a quick guess and picked the one that I was closest to.

It could have been minutes or hours later, all I knew was that it was still dark when I developed a jabbing pain in my right shoulder, not enough to cause worry but enough to wake me up. The root of my discomfort came from what appeared to be a silhouette of a tall thin woman, with a French accent. She claimed, in a mixture of French and English, that among other things she was the resident of the bed I was in. Trying to roll over and ignore her, I hoped she'd either take my empty bed or join me, if she really wanted her own mattress so badly. She wasn't giving in so easily and turned the light on, insisting on waking up the entire room with her angry babble.

She may have been right but the bright light wasn't going to help any of us sleep, so I just crawled out of her bunk and across the floor to the other vacant bed, trying my best to take her sheet with me. I couldn't get back to sleep though as my bladder had also woken up during the commotion. Getting up and stumbling out of the door in only my boxers I headed down the corridor and found the toilet with relative ease, only to discover on my return that my bedroom door had locked itself, despite my efforts to leave it open. Without a choice, I began knocking at the door, wondering how my roommates would react to being woken up yet again. When no one replied to the first gentle taps, I stepped it up a notch with a series of harder thuds. Finally, after what seemed like ten minutes of knocking while I stood out in the corridor in only my underwear, the door opened.

'Matt? *Fuck*, is it that time already?' Ryan slurred as he stood in the doorway after kindly opening it.

'No, I don't think so... what are you doing in my dorm? I thought you were in a different one,' I mumbled.

'This is *my* room buddy, I think yours is next door,' he answered, looking down the corridor where my own door still stood partially open.

'Oh bollocks, sorry Ryan. Get some sleep mate, we've got a long drive tomorrow and you look like shit,' I muttered, before making my way back down the corridor.

When even more nudging and poking abruptly ended my latest sleeping effort, I had visions behind closed eyelids of yet another person telling me to get out of their bed and so tried to ignore it until it became unbearable.

'*Matt*, time to get up, we were meant to have left about two hours ago. The couple that are coming with us were up and ready to go on time and seem to have been getting a little stressed out I think,' Scott said, kneeling beside my bed and looking just as bad as I felt. '*Shit, really*? Okay, give me ten minutes,' I mumbled, before turning back over and piecing together how I'd come to be in such a state.

Minutes later the bright sun blinded me, making my headache worse, as I rounded the corner of the hostel looking for the others. The previous day, the car had been highly regarded by Ryan, as though it was a road demon capable of both light speed and time travel, which left me stumped when I saw the dirty bluish-white car parked awkwardly against the curb, with the back sticking out into the road into which he was loading bags. Reading my bemused expression, Ryan stepped forward to take my bag, 'Let me introduce you to my baby, she's an eighty-four Bluebird and known affectionately to all as *The Viagra Mobile*,' Ryan said, beaming with pride.

'Viagra Mobile?' I repeated, before noticing a weathered sticker planted discreetly next to a rust spot, and probably covering up a larger one, with the tag line, *Viagra is for pussies*.

'It's a fine looking automobile Ryan. If you think it'll deliver us to Byron then I'm willing to believe.'

'Don't worry buddy it'll be fine,' he replied, trying to squash my backpack into the already crowded boot.

Peering into the empty back seat, I could see an imitation leopard skin seat cover stretched across, giving the car the feel that it belonged in a low budget porn flick, rather than on the roads. I was just on the verge of climbing in when I saw Scott rounding the corner with the couple. I smiled in anticipation of meeting my fellow passengers, but as they got closer the smile dropped, replaced by shock as I realised one half of the couple was Claire. Speechless, I watched as her own smile faded and she recognised me, her eyes full of panic as she silently mouthed, '*Shit!*' Considering that in my mind, she was rotting in a prison, she looked surprisingly good but as much as I wanted to find out exactly what had happened, I knew I couldn't do anything more than bite my tongue and pretend I didn't know her.

The boyfriend was none other than *the boyfriend,* Brent, a couple of inches taller than myself, with broad shoulders and short-styled hair. The collar on his rugby shirt was turned up and he wore a pair of knee length khaki shorts and leather sandals. As we shook hands, I couldn't believe the situation I was in. Claire too, thankfully, acted like a total stranger, as we both threw questioning glances at one another whenever Brent's back was turned.

Getting in the car, an image of Brent falling asleep while Claire and I caught up for lost time on the porn rug flashed in and quickly back out of my mind, the fantasy blown as Brent slid into the middle seat, dividing us both. He, unlike some of us in the car, was blatantly not hung-over, nor was he sympathetic to those who were and as we slowly headed out of the city and I tried my best to continue my desperately needed sleep, Brent had other ideas for helping me passing the time. He must have mistaken my weary, red-eyed appearance for that of a bored man in need of a good chat and so began an endless sea of questions from him, all the while I was as vague as I could be, in a futile attempt to show my exhaustion. An hour later and out of the city, I heard Scott snoring and looked over to see Claire asleep, so I decided to stop being polite and made my excuses, turning away from him and pressing my thumping head up against the vibrating window.

It must have been about ten-thirty, when I woke up, my face still pressed up against the hot window. Through closed eyes I began to ponder the real likelihood of Claire's appearance, and wondered if in fact it was just a horrible figment of my imagination. Cautiously turning around, hoping it was all in my mind, I received a small fright to see Brent smiling back at me, Claire still asleep on his other side.

As if making up for lost time, Brent immediately started talking, this time about Claire and himself. Some of what he was telling me I already knew, but what I didn't know was that they had just enjoyed a few days together in Thailand after Brent had romantically turned up to surprise his love, although he failed to mention anything about finding her in a dingy prison. Ryan, listening quietly to our conversation, hadn't clicked onto the fact that my Claire and Brent's Claire were one and the same person. He intervened into the one sided conversation, 'Matt, didn't you say that you were on that island with some girl, but she got arrested and you got robbed the day after the full moon party?' he said, as Claire's eyes opened and she glanced over Brent's shoulder towards me with an evil stare.

'Yeah... I did,' I replied, wanting to leave the conversation alone and trying to avoid Claire's gaze. I could sense that Brent was about to ask me a question, when Ryan broke the silence announcing a stop at a garage.

Climbing out of the car, Claire and Brent headed into the shop together while I hung back with Ryan and Scott, who were filling up the tank.

'Guys, you won't believe this but the girl who got arrested - Claire, is this Claire, the one in the back seat,' I quickly explained, as I watched them take in my words.

'What, the one that was arrested?' Scott asked.

'Yeah, well, no. Obviously she wasn't arrested but regardless, this is her.'

'Holy shit buddy, that's *fucked*,' Ryan said, 'what are you going to do?'

'Well, there's not much I can do, not until we get to Byron at least, I just thought you'd better know, before anyone puts their foot in it again,' I said, looking at Ryan, as the petrol pump clicked to a stop.

Ten minutes later we were back on the road, having stocked up on drinks and snacks. Brent remained in the middle seat and continued his incessant talking. Then the conversation moved to our accommodation plans in Byron Bay. Ryan and Scott had booked into a hostel called The Reef House and when I mentioned that I was meant to be staying at Liquid Dreams, Brent happily piped up that he and Claire were also staying there.

'We could be neighbours Matt,' he beamed.

'Yeah, *maybe* Brent,' I replied, with a lot less enthusiasm.

'Wow, maybe you and Brent could help Matt get himself another lady for New Year, after all the shit that happened to him in Thailand, huh Claire?' Scott added, throwing Claire a quick wink before smiling at me, hoping I'd appreciate the joke.

'Thanks Scott,' I bitterly replied, seeing the funny side but hoping he'd shut up.

'I reckon we'll be able to find him someone, don't you think babe?' Brent said, looking over to Claire who'd been staring at me with an intense hatred.

'Yeah,' she shakily replied.

We sat in silence for a long period after that just watching the Australian landscape whizz by. It wasn't anything too exciting, only trees and bushes, certainly not as dramatic as the huge limestone pinnacles that I'd passed on the road to Koh Phi Phi. It had been hours since our last stop, already coming up to four o'clock, when Ryan announced we were running low on petrol.

Pulling into the forecourt I felt as if we were in the outback. It was just a small place with a couple of rusty pumps and a basic shop fronting a garage with a dilapidated tow truck parked outside. Inside, a tall, thin woman with her front teeth missing and short jet-black hair, stood behind the counter. She took no notice of us when we entered the shop, lost in her magazine. As Brent disappeared back outside, looking for the toilet, I took my opportunity to be alone with Claire. '*So...* care to tell me what the *fuck* happened back on the island?' I asked, my words coming out stronger than I'd meant, although not anywhere as harsh as I'd been rehearsing in my mind all day. Claire, pursing her lips and pondering her words, finally spoke. 'What do you think happened? Brent turned up, the big idiot,' she said.

'Oh, *oh well*, that explains it all. So I got back the next morning, the door had been shouldered in, your bags gone, my little bag gone, of course I should have guessed it was all because of your psycho boyfriend. How stupid of me,' I said.

'I thought you'd done that to the door, because you'd lost your key? Look, I left you on the dance floor, came back and you were gone. Then I got a text from Brent saying he was at the party, where was I? So I had no option but to go back to our room and hope you were there, although you'd obviously been back already as the door was open and your stuff was all scattered about. So I hid out for the rest of the night in our room, unable to sleep from the pills, before I took my things and left to find Brent in the morning. So what happened to you that night?' she asked.

'If you really want to know what happened...' I started, interrupted by the shop door opening again and Brent walking back in. Instantly, Claire turned away and fell silent.

Back in the car we hadn't even been driving for a minute, when we began to slow down to a halt on the side of the road.

'What's up, did you forget something?' Ryan asked Scott who was now driving for the first time that day.

'No bud, the car just lost all power,' Scott said, turning around to face us with a worried look.

'That's not funny man, come on it's Christmas Eve, good joke but let's get cracking,' Ryan replied, but I could see by Scott's face that he wasn't messing around.

'I'm serious man, the Viagra Mobile has just gone limp,' Scott sadly explained.

'Who knows anything about cars...? Someone?' Ryan asked, getting out and lifting up the bonnet.

'I can't even drive,' I said.

'I can change a tyre and check the oil, but that's about it, sorry,' Brent said.

'*Sorry guys*, me neither,' Claire added. So we did all we knew how to do and checked the water and oil levels, but both seemed fine.

'Try and start it again, maybe it'll work all right now,' Scott suggested, which Ryan did, only to be rewarded with an awful churning noise for his efforts.

'*Shit*,' Scott dismally groaned, 'I guess we could take it back to that garage,' he said as Ryan got back out of the car.

'What, the shitty one back there?' Brent questioned, clearly disapproving.

'Yeah, they had a tow truck, maybe they can fix it,' Ryan said.

'This has got to be a joke guys, I *need* to get to Byron soon, its nearly Christmas and I'm not about to spend it standing by the road side,' Claire selfishly ranted, lighting up a cigarette.

'The garage it is,' I added, agreeing with the Canadians. 'Let's go.'

Grabbing our valuables out of the car, we followed Ryan's speedy march towards the garage. Trying to calm the situation down by telling ourselves it was just something simple and within half an hour we'd be back on the road, *guaranteed*. Ten minutes of trudging along the roadside under the scorching afternoon sun and we were back at the garage.

Walking inside the shop, the assistant looked up from her magazine, in disbelief. 'What can I do for youse?' she asked, sensing we hadn't just come in for a pack of gum. As Ryan spoke up and took charge, telling her about the car problem, the mechanic must have been eavesdropping through a door, because he burst through with a dopey smile and presented himself. He was a gangly guy, bearing a slight resemblance to the woman but with an oily brown mullet, dirty overalls and a grubby bandage on his right hand.

'G'day guys, so I heard you got some car trouble?' he asked, in a broad Australian accent. Listening as Ryan repeated himself, the mechanic crossed his arms and gave a little smirk, 'Ah yeah mate, that's shit luck. Ya know I'd love to help ya but I've finished me work 'til Jan now…' he said, pausing for effect, as we all stood shocked, 'but I can see ya in a bind, so I'll help but with overtime fees ya know.'

'*Right,*' Ryan replied, sounding deflated. The mechanic, seeing an opportunity to make a quick buck, ran his greasy hand through his already mucky hair.

'Well 'op in the truck mate and we'll tow her back, maybe it's just some-in simple and you can get back on the road again, yeah,' the mechanic said, as he gestured at Ryan to follow him.

We watched as the rusty pick-up vanished down the road in a wheelspinning dust cloud, leaving us to concoct a backup plan. Byron Bay was only about four hours or so away, which in Australia was the equivalent of the next town along, so we figured that with any luck we might be able to hitch a ride the rest of the way. Beyond that, it would be a Christmas in redneck Australia at the garage with our two new friends.

Ten minutes later both Ryan and the Viagra Mobile were back, although woefully it was being towed. Unhooking and pushing the car into the garage, we all huddled around the engine, as we waited for the mechanic to come and fix it. Before he did anything, he grabbed a bottle of beer from the garage fridge and proceeded to walk around the car, eyeing it up and shaking his head grimly, before stopping and crouching down to peer in at the engine.

After minutes of pottering around and fiddling, he turned to Ryan with a grave expression and announced the cam belt had gone. 'When the cam goes, the engine's stuffed,' he explained. 'Now I *could* fix it *but* I don't have the parts and wouldn't be able to get 'em until the New Year, it is Christmas ya know?'

'What about towing it to Byron Bay?' Scott asked.

'Byron? Strewth, you gotta be yanking my chain, that ain't just down the road mate,' he said, taking a long swig of his beer.

'Well can we get another garage to tow it?' Scott asked.

'Mate, you may not have noticed, but we're as scarce as teeth on a hen round here. Look you can pay me four hundred dollars to park it here until New Year if ya like, then I'll fix it good and proper.'

'Four hundred dollars?' Ryan exclaimed.

'Or if ya don't wanna come back for it, I'll take it to a scrappers for four-fifty,' the mechanic smiled.

'Right,' Ryan started, 'well looks like I've got a problem here Chief, I don't have four hundred dollars to leave the car here and nor do I have four-fifty to scrap it... So, I reckon we'll have to push it to the roadside and I'll come back for it after New Year and get it fixed when you *do* have the parts. *How's that?*' Ryan smiled, thinking he had it all figured out.

'Nah mate, you must have a few kangaroos loose in the paddock, you can't do that. If you leave it on the roadside, the cops will come and tow it away, costing you a lot more than four hundred. If you really don't have the money, I'll take the car off your hands, although I wouldn't be able to pay you anything for it,' the mechanic said, as he pulled another bottle of beer out of the garage fridge.

'Let me get this straight, you want me to sign the car over to you for free? No way man this car cost me eight hundred bucks,' Ryan argued. 'She's my baby and I'm not about to just *hand* it over to you.'

Sensing that Ryan was getting livid, Scott grabbed his shoulder and suggested we all go outside and talk it over. As the car belonged to Ryan we knew it had to be his choice but we also knew the longer we spent at the garage the harder it was going to be to get to Byron Bay.

'Look Ryan, this greasy bastard has got you over a barrel. If you haven't got the money I don't see what else you can do,' Scott said, saying what we were all thinking, as my phone beeped in my pocket.

'Fine, so what now?' Ryan asked.

'Lets just beat the shit out of him, it'll make us feel better,' Brent suggested, looking even more outraged than Ryan.

'Don't be stupid Brent!' Claire snapped, grabbing his arm.

'Get a beer and hitch,' I said, reading those exact words off my phone, as Lola's solution to my transport problem finally came through over a day later.

'Get a beer and hitch?' Ryan asked.

'Yeah, why not? The mechanic's got beers. Let's get some and get moving,' Scott said.

'What and hand the car over for free?' Ryan asked.

'Swap it for five beers,' Claire said, smiling at the absurdity of trading a car for beer.

'Okay... *Okay*, yeah why the fuck not,' Ryan said, walking back into the garage.

Minutes later, beers in hand, under the weight of our bags, we hit the road towards Byron Bay again, this time on foot. As soon as we were out of sight from the garage we all stopped and began to discuss who should go first, should we be able to hitch a ride. Everyone had his or her arguments regarding who should be the first to go and talking about it was just heightening our already frayed tempers, so we all agreed on a more diplomatic system. Ryan pulled his dog-eared pack of playing cards out from his backpack and we all agreed to pick a card, with the highest going first and lowest last. Claire, of course, for safety's sake, was exempt from this and agreed to go in the first car with two spaces no matter whom she went with. So it was agreed that Brent should go first with his Queen of clubs. Next to travel would be myself with a ten of spades. The Canadians each produced a red two leaving them to patiently wait until last and argue it over among themselves, should there only be one space.

As the odd few cars flew by, I began to wonder what kind of freaks might be out there to pick us all up. This was, I knew, the subject of numerous horror movies. They always started innocently enough, and there was always a couple hitching. So that would mean I would need Claire along in the car too, in an effort to do the required screaming. Thankfully, the more that I thought about it, the more it turned around in my mind to me arriving into Byron Bay unscathed after a hellish adventure, hand in hand with Claire. She would then dump Brent, if he'd survived, just in time for us to spend a romantic Christmas together.

As my mind continued to wander, and the beers dried up, bitching about our situation broke out and gave me a welcome distraction. Ryan started off moaning about only having received a measly few beers in exchange for his pride and joy. Scott on the other hand moaned straight back at him, about the mechanic being such a dick and not even offering us a lift anywhere. Brent started with his own complaints, directed towards Claire for stopping him from beating the mechanic up, who in turn faced Ryan and began insulting his car. I, on the other hand, wanted to curse Ryan for not checking his car was up to the journey before we'd left, frustrated at the prospect of spending my first Christmas abroad in the sticks. However, given how bad Ryan had taken the whole thing and how highly strung we all were, I decided to remain silent and try to remain positive.

It had been nearly half an hour of thumbing and cursing, when the first car pulled up. All five of us were still there, so we knew it was Brent's ride if not Claire's too. The car was a dirty light-blue coloured estate, with a few small dents around it and a red bonnet, looking as though it was from the same family tree as the late Viagra Mobile. On the roof were two surfboards and as far as we could see only the driver inside. We all stepped up to the open window, following the sweet smell of hashish that was wafting out of it, followed by a head, with long blond locks that hung in front of his face as he casually looked us all up and down.

'How you doin' guys? Where you headed?' he asked, his accent sounding similar to Ryan's and Scott's, as Brent stepped up and leant in a bit closer.

'Byron Bay, or anywhere in that direction,' he said, as the driver looked around at us all, took a puff of the diminishing joint and smiled.

'I'm heading to Byron dude, what are there?' he asked, 'Five people? No worries, if you don't mind sitting on one another then hop in,' he merrily said. Glancing from one person to the next and back again, we collectively shrugged and agreed, '*Okay.*'

Stepping out of the car to open up the boot, our driver was barefoot, wearing a pair of baggy blue shorts and an unbuttoned stripy shirt, with straight blond hair that hung just over his stoned eyes. 'Hi, I'm Josh,' he said as he greeted us all, with a friendly smile.

No one seemed to mind that Josh was a little stoned, as we all knew it was either that or potentially spend the rest of the night on the side of the road. Cramming our bags in the boot the best we could, I saw the opportunity for the vacant front seat and sneaked inside whilst the others were making small talk with Josh. Already on the front seat were a skateboard, a couple of surf magazines and a pile of crisp packets and empty drink bottles. Fitting the skateboard between my legs, I pushed the rest onto the floor and looked back to see the others squashed up, with Brent bearing the weight of Claire on his lap. Beside him the Canadians were also squashed, each with a big backpack on their lap. As we pulled away I began to feel a sense of victory. Although I hadn't admitted it, the prospect of hitching alone for my first ever time, with all the murderous freaks about, to a town I didn't know was definitely a daunting one. At least the five of us were all together and Josh seemed too mellow and caned to possibly want to murder us.

As we started talking, we learnt that Josh, nineteen years old, was over from California, backpacking and surfing through Australia alone. In Byron Bay he was intending to sleep in the car for two weeks rather than paying out the extortionate price of a dorm bed. Earlier in the year, he'd already spent over four months in Byron Bay, having left briefly to explore more of the East Coast and renew his visa with a little time surfing in Fiji. Explaining our recent ordeal, Josh found it hilarious that we'd swapped a car for a few bottles of beer, his chuckle lightening our sour mood for the first time since the beer had been drunk.

As we trundled into Byron Bay and down the main street, it was now seven o'clock and we were only two hours behind our original schedule, had we departed Sydney at five as planned. Staring out of the window, I tried to take in as much of the town as I could. Low rise buildings and trees lined the road, the pavements busy with an eclectic mix of hippies, surfers and backpackers.

'Wow, it's so much busier than a few weeks ago,' Josh commented. 'So Ryan and Scott, you're at Reef House, yeah?' he asked.

'Yeah, it's just down here on the left,' Scott said.

'I remember, I woke up there once, *man* that was a crazy night,' Josh said, mostly for his own benefit. 'If it's cool with you, I'll drop you guys off first, I need to catch up with an old pal at Liquid Dreams while I'm there,' he said.

'Sure, hey do you guys fancy meeting for some beers later on?' Scott asked.

'I think we're going to have a quiet dinner and an early night, I'm exhausted,' Claire said.

'I'm keen,' I replied 'I'll meet you at yours at nine, is that alright?' I asked, although wondering if I'd also get a chance to catch up with Lola and Noodle.

Driving just seconds around the corner, we spotted the hand painted sign for Liquid Dreams Backpackers' Hostel. As we got our things together Josh also unstrapped his two surfboards, putting one inside the car and carrying the other up the stairs with us to the reception. Behind the counter stood what appeared to be an older version of Josh, with similar long locks, except in silver, and almost identical clothes of baggy shorts and an unbuttoned short sleeved shirt. In fact, until the old man spoke and revealed an Australian accent, I was thinking it might be Josh's dad.

'Hey Josh, it's been a while mate. How did the new board go?' the old man asked, as he picked up Josh's surfboard, inspecting it.

'Ah, Steve, it was so sweet dude, perfect for Fiji. I was actually hoping I might be able to store it here for a bit as I'm going to ride my six-two until the waves pick up,' Josh replied, hugging the old man and as far as I could tell, talking about surf.

'No worries, have you heard from Issi these past few days?' Steve asked.

'No, I left my phone out during a storm in Fiji, it's not been working right since. Why, is she okay?'

'She's fine mate, there's a party tonight at her house,' Steve said, acknowledging Claire, Brent and myself for the first time, 'Sorry guys, I'll be right with you,' he said.

'Ah sweet, I'm there. Hey do you mind if I take a quick shower? It's either that or a swim in the sea,' Josh asked.

'Knock yourself out mate, I'll catch you at the party later on,' Steve said.

'Hey nice to meet you all, enjoy Byron,' Josh called out as he ran off in search of a towel, leaving Steve holding his board.

'Okay guys, checking in I guess. What are your names?' Steve asked.

As he processed Claire and Brent first, taking them upstairs to their room, I took a moment to check out the communal notice board. All manner of things were up for sale from IPods to cars, but one particular advert caught my eye, offering a surfboard for sale, *ideal for beginners*, it read. As I began to ponder buying a board, I heard a door open and turned to see a familiar face.

'Matt!' Noodle shouted as he walked into the reception, beer in hand.

'Damn, Lola told me you were having problems getting here, we were beginning to think you wouldn't make it. Did you get her text?' he asked.

'Yeah, I did,' I said, shaking Noodle's hand, 'I got a beer and hitched as she suggested,' I replied, deciding to play it cool and not make an issue of her rather delayed and useless response.

'Hey Steve!' Noodle called out as the old man returned. 'Have you met my mate Matt?' Noodle said, as Steve got closer.

'Ah! *You're* the one who was stuck for a ride? Well, looks like you did alright in the end, if you came with Josh. The name's Steve, nice to meet you mate,' he said, shaking my hand.

'Matt, when you're done checking in, come up to the veranda and grab a beer, we're all heading out to a house party in a bit, so don't take too long,' Noodle said, 'Hey, Steve, you're coming along too right?' he asked.

'Yeah, I'll be there. Some of us have to work though, so I'll be along a little later,' Steve replied, 'Okay, Matt. Well… welcome to Byron Bay, looks like you picked a hell of a night to arrive. Let me show you to your room,' he said, leading me down a corridor.

Seven

Emerging from a refreshing shower I wandered back into my brightly painted room, which, judging by the six beds and stacks of surfboards in the corners, I was sharing with a few surfers. Putting on some clean clothes, I followed Noodle's instructions and headed upstairs to a large wooden veranda that stretched around the building and housed a dozen or so candlelit tables. Walking around looking for Noodle, everyone was in good spirits with quite a few Santa hats being worn, looking at complete odds with the summer clothes and warm weather.

I found Noodle sat alone, rolling a cigarette, box of beer on the table in front of him, his eyes lit up as I approached, 'Matt, just in time, everyone else headed off to the party a couple of minutes ago,' he said, passing me a cold bottle of beer.

'Cool, thanks… cheers,' I said, unscrewing the top of the beer and knocking my bottle into his. 'Is there any chance of grabbing a quick bite to eat, I'm starving?' I asked.

'Yeah, well, there will be a barbie at the party, I'm sure you'll be able to grab something there,' he said.

'Alright, let's go then,' I said, Noodle already standing up and picking up the beers. Following him down the stairs, I stopped briefly at the notice board beside the reception.

'I saw this ad earlier, for a long board, says it's perfect for beginners, what do you think?' I asked.

'What do I think about a long board being ideal for beginners or what do I think about you buying one?' he asked, as we headed out of the backpackers and across the road.

'Both.'

'I think they're good for beginners, easy to catch waves on and pretty stable, I don't think you should buy one though,' he stated.

'Why not? I'm serious about wanting to learn,' I replied.

'I know, but if you're planning to travel around Oz for the next year then you need something a little more compact. A long board will be a nightmare to lug around. I guarantee that's the only reason the board's up for sale, the owner realised it too late,' he said. 'If you want to buy a good beginner board, then I'll help you pick one that will be a little more practical and still good for learning on. For the time being Steve might have something knocking around that you could start on, have a chat with him at the party tonight.'

As our conversation ended, I realised we'd reached the party. Ahead of us, in what seemed like it should be a quiet residential street, loud music was thumping out of a small box-like one-storey house, with a garden almost double its size where around twenty people were either sat or stood around, lanterns and candles dotted about providing light.

Walking into the garden I could see Josh on the other side chatting to a couple of guys. I scanned the crowd for Lola but she was nowhere to be seen. Upon registering Noodle's presence, seemingly half of the party suddenly broke away from their conversations and approached him, swamping him with hugs and kisses, as though he was the prodigal son returning.

'Noodle, good to see you mate, Steve told me you were back, though I heard a rumour we'd almost lost you for a bit. Awesome to see you alive and well,' a towering guy, with a bushy brown beard said, as he gave Noodle a big hug.

'Thanks Ron,' Noodle said, his eyes sparkling and grin huge, as he handed the box of beer over to me and turned to see the next well-wisher.

As I stood watching him for a moment, I could see more of the old Noodle returning. Deciding to look for Lola and drop off the beer, I headed into the small house. Inside there was a tiny lounge, which I suspected doubled as a bedroom, as I noticed a couple of mattresses and a dozen cushions on the floor, but no sofa. There was no sign of a television either, just a small stereo which was hooked up to an Ipod, playing an old Foo Fighters song. Colourful sarongs were hung up on the walls and in one corner stood a small surfboard that had obviously been in a few scrapes, with a patchwork of repairs and dents across its belly. To the left was a wide opening into a poky kitchen, and a door that I guessed was for the bathroom.

There were ten people crammed inside, four of them sat on cushions taking turns trying to play a didgeridoo, sporadically bursting out into fits of laughter at their attempts, the others stood around chatting between the living room and kitchen. As I nervously walked in, the woman closest to the door noticed me entering and came over.

Looking no older than twenty, the woman was stunning. She was wearing a red flowery dress and her jet-black hair, which fell down across her deeply tanned, bare shoulders, was pinned back on

101

one side with a small red flower. Like most of the others in the house, she too was barefoot, with a blue and white beaded anklet around her right ankle.

'Hi, how are you? I don't think we've met, I'm Isabella,' she said with a strong Spanish accent.

'Hi, no, I don't think we have,' I said, desperately trying to think of something interesting to say as I shook her hand, but all I could manage was, 'I'm Matt.'

'*Right*, so who are you here with?' she asked.

'Noodle,' I replied.

'Noodle? Oh okay, yeah, loads of people have been talking about him these past few days, I don't think I've met him either. Didn't he nearly die in a surfing accident?'

'Well, kind of, he had a bad session in Indo,' I said, using Noodle's expression for Indonesia.

'Yeah, that's what I heard. Wow, I'd love to meet him,' she replied.

'He's around somewhere... so am I right in thinking there's a barbie on the go?' I asked.

'Yeah there will be, I think Josh was going to be in charge of it. Hang on,' she said, calling Josh over.

'Hey, dude,' Josh said to me as he came over, hand in hand with a petite young Australian woman, who was barefoot and wearing a long flowing gypsy skirt and small jewelled bindi on her forehead. 'You sure don't waste any time, minutes in town and already found a party, good skills dude,' he said.

'Do you guys know each other?' Isabella asked.

'Sure do Issi, this is one of the guys I picked up earlier, swapped his car for a beer,' Josh said. 'Sorry I've forgotten your name dude?'

'It's Matt,' I replied, my focus on Isabella. 'Are you Issi, as in this is your party?' I asked her.

'Sure am,' she smiled. 'Have you met Ambur?' she said, introducing me to the woman on Josh's arm, as we shook hands.

'So Josh, do you think you and... Matt here, could grab yourselves some beer from the kitchen and get the barbie going? Ambur and I need a chat,' Isabella said with a naughty smile, as Josh and I nodded in agreement.

Following Josh back out into the garden towards the barbeque, I noticed Lola had arrived and was standing beside Noodle, meeting his old friends. Chatting to Josh as we waited for the charcoal to heat up, I found out that Ambur was his on-off girlfriend, a born and bred local of Byron Bay whose parents had emigrated from India in the seventies. She worked as the manager in an organic café in the town and knew the area inside out. Over the months that Josh had spent in the small town, it was clear he'd made a lot of friends and I began to understand his reluctance to get away and explore more of the country.

Leaving Josh with the barbeque whilst I went in search of more beer, I made a detour to Lola who upon seeing me, broke away from the group huddled around Noodle, listening to his stories.

'Hey Matt, I see you made it okay then,' she stated as we hugged. 'We got in last night, seems Noodle knows most of the town! So I don't suppose you've seen much of Byron yet have you?' she asked.

'Only from the car coming in, but so far so good. It's really quite odd to think it's Christmas Eve and we're stood around in shorts, cooking a barbeque,' I said, spotting Isabella coming out of the house. 'Have you met Isabella yet?' I asked Lola, whilst catching Isabella's eye.

'No, I don't think I have, hi,' Isabella said to Lola before turning to me. 'How's the barbie coming along?'

'It's nearly there, Josh's got it under control, I'm on beer duty,' I answered.

'Cool, well there's a bin full of beer and ice in the kitchen, help yourself,' she said, staying to talk to Lola as I went inside.

Digging my left hand deep down into the ice filled waters of the beer bin, like an adults' lucky dip, I pulled out three small bottles of VB. Dropping one bottle off to Lola, who was still chatting to Isabella, I took the other bottles over to the barbeque handing one to Josh.

'So how long have you been surfing for?' I asked him, as we started putting the meat on the grill.

'For more of my life than I haven't been,' he responded, 'My parents were surfing back in the sixties, so it's kind of a family thing, I guess. My little bro and sis both rip too. How about you?' he asked.

'Never tried it but Noodle reckoned I might be able to borrow a board off Steve and maybe go out tomorrow,' I said

'Okay, yeah. It's supposed to be pretty small tomorrow, so it'll be good for learning. I'd be happy to give you a few pointers in the water too if you like?' he offered.

'Really? That would be great, thanks,' I said.

'No sweat, you're mates with Noodle is that right?' Josh asked.

'Yeah, do you know him?'

'No, but I know of him. From what I heard he went a bit cuckoo in Indo, surfing over a dry reef,' Josh said.

'Yeah, I think it's been a pretty rough year for him.' I said.

'I heard he lost his girlfriend. Apparently she died surfing in England, he'd not been out with her and the guilt fucked him right up,' Josh solemnly nodded. 'Okay, I reckon this food's ready. Come and get it!' he shouted, stealing everyone's attention, their chilled expressions suddenly turning into ravenous carnivores.

'Make sure you keep a veggie burger for Ambur, she'll kill me if it all goes,' Josh requested, as we started dishing the food out.

Turning up in time for the last burger, Steve grabbed himself a beer and joined a few of us sat around the cushions in the lounge. Although nothing had been said, it now seemed pretty evident that Noodle and Lola had become an item, as she lay across a few cushions resting her head on his chest. Similarly Josh and Ambur were also wrapped up in each other, leaving myself, Steve and Isabella dotted about on the other cushions. Watching Isabella get up to mingle with some of her other guests, I couldn't help but feel mesmerised by her. She was, as it turned out, only nineteen but seemed so much more switched on than I felt, with fourteen months of travelling already under her belt, backpacking alone through South America and across to Australia, where she'd admittedly gotten a little stuck, running out of money and desire to leave.

As Steve began recalling the account of his surfing adventures in Senegal during the eighties, I could tell it was a story he'd told a thousand times before, but by the gleam in his eye and excitement in his voice, it felt like he was reliving a memory of an event from only yesterday. As he finished, I was prompted to explain how five of us had come to be in the middle of nowhere hitching a ride, when Josh had come along. I was hoping that I was telling the story with at least half of Steve's passion but just as I got to the point of explaining the awkward situation of Claire and I sharing the back seat with her boyfriend, thankful that Isabella wasn't around to hear it, I suddenly remembered that I was meant to have been meeting the Canadians over an hour earlier. Cursing myself whilst continuing with the story, I couldn't help feeling racked with guilt that they would think I was abandoning them now that I'd used them for the lift to town.

Handing us all new beers and returning to our circle with a small bag of weed and skins, Isabella sat down and began rolling our first joint of the evening.

'I think we may need to move the party down to the beach in a bit,' Isabella said, as she glanced up from the task at hand. 'Our neighbours have got little kids who'll probably be lying awake listening to our party, worried that Santa might visit us first and get stuck at our party,' she smiled. 'Besides which they'll probably complain to my landlady again, which I really don't need,' she added.

'Fair enough, do you need a hand clearing up stuff?' I asked, surprising myself by the offer.

'Okay, yeah. I'm not going to worry too much about the place tonight but if you can clear up the beer bottles from the garden and just put them in the kitchen, that would be great. There's no immediate rush though,' she said, as I made a move to stand up. 'Let's smoke this first and then think more about going.'

With twenty pairs of hands helping to clear up, we were done almost instantly. Those who were moving onto the beach were then given a new task, to take a handful from the pile of branches Isabella had pilled in a corner of the garden.

'I'm just going to get some doughnuts from the bakery, I'll meet you guys down the beach at the usual spot yeah?' Josh announced as we began filling our hands up. 'Anyone want anything or fancy a walk into town?' he asked, looking for company.

'I'm going to help Issi, if that's okay,' Ambur said as she carried a stray beer bottle into the kitchen.

'I'll come,' I said, glancing over to Isabella. 'Is that alright? I mean with the wood and that?' I asked her, eager for my first taste of the town but not wanting to leave them short on wood.

'I think we'll manage, just as long as you get me a brownie,' she replied, picking up a handful of branches.

'Ooh, brownie for me too!' Ambur called out from the kitchen.

'Can you get me some doughnuts, as well?' Noodle asked before, eight others put in their orders, causing us to write a list.

Dreadlocks and Santa hats passed us by in a smiling blur as we crossed onto the main road. It seemed the spirit of Christmas had cast a spell on the town. Strangers walked by wishing us a *Merry Christmas*, others were spontaneously dancing and twirling poi on the pavement. The only thing missing from a fairytale Christmas was the snow.

'This road right here, Jonson Street, is pretty much the epicentre of Byron Bay,' Josh pointed out, waving to a couple of girls across the road. 'From here it stretches right down to the beach, where there's a surf break called *the wreck*. If you go in the other direction you'll find Liquid Dreams and the supermarket.'

'Is the wreck the best place to surf then?' I asked.

'It's okay for beginners, so we might go there tomorrow but there are much better breaks around the bay with the right conditions,' he said.

'Shit, that reminds me, I haven't asked Steve for a board yet. Do you think he'll mind?'

'Nah, I'm sure it'll be fine, Steve's a good guy and he's got plenty of boards knocking around. Just watch it with the doughnuts tonight, the sharks are attracted to the scent,' he said, with a serious tone.

'Sharks! Are there sharks here?' I asked, feeling my heart beginning to pound, and stopping me in my paces. 'I'm not surfing in shark infested water!'

'Dude,' he laughed, 'if you want to surf you're going to have to get used to the idea that we're not alone in the water. Yeah, there are sharks here but there are also dolphins, whales and fish. Besides no one's been attacked for years, I've been surfing here for months and have never even seen a shark here.'

'Oh great, I feel so much better,' I sarcastically offered. 'Probably means Byron's about due an attack if it's been a while,' I said, trying to relax but still feeling a little tense, with images of sharks and blood filling my mind.

'Well, tomorrow I'll keep an eye out for you so you can concentrate on surfing without worrying,' he said.

'Okay thanks.'

'And if you see me paddling past you at lightning speed, I wouldn't hang about in the water,' he laughed.

'Well that's great I feel so much safer now, thanks Josh,' I said, smiling and joining in with the joke.

On the way to the bakery Josh gave me a guided tour of the town, pointing out the pubs, clubs, surf shops and the best takeaway restaurants. As we kept going, I thought I heard my name being called out, only to turn around and see only strangers. Moments later, I felt a hand on my shoulder and whirled around to discover Ryan and Scott merrily stood behind us.

'Hey buddy, isn't this town great?' Ryan said, opening his arms out and trying to embrace it all.

'Hi guys, how you doing?' Josh asked.

'Oh man, I love this town, there are beautiful people everywhere,' Scott said.

'It's cool huh? Sorry that I didn't come around earlier, I... I got a bit caught up,' I apologised.

'No problem, you didn't miss much, we just grabbed a bit of food and a few beers. Do you fancy coming to a club?' Ryan asked.

'No, I don't think so, were just going to the bakery before heading down to the beach for a little party, you're welcome to join us if you like?' I replied, hoping I could make up for forgetting about them earlier, but as Ryan looked at Scott for an answer, their attention was captured by a group of women headed towards town.

'Sounds good Matt, but I think I'm following them,' Scott said, his gaze focused in the direction of the women. 'Although if there's a bakery open, I'm starving,' he added.

'Yeah, good call, pastries then club,' Ryan smiled, as we continued walking.

The bakery, Josh pointed out, was an institution in Byron Bay. Open twenty-four hours a day, its business particularly boomed during the early hours when the inevitable munchies would kick in throughout the town. The stoners' equivalent to the British kebab shop that fed the drunk into the early hours of the morning. Except with the bakery, there was no risk of waking up with a rancid kebab taste in your mouth.

It was at the bakery that the four of us inadvertently found ourselves standing in the long queue with Brent and Claire. Both drunk, they were all smiles to see us and for a moment we were reunited, and again, in search of the same thing. Brent didn't stay with us for long, buckling to nature's call he left Claire with an order and his wallet before vanishing into the crowd.

No sooner had I watched Brent go, when Claire took us all by surprise and stepped forward, threw her arms around me and planted her lips on my own. As I pushed her away, tasting the tobacco on her breath, all I could think about was Brent and how angry he would be, but as she held tight I relaxed a little. As she pulled away the kiss began to feel almost right, until I realised that her smiling face wasn't the one I wanted to see. I stole a glance at the others who were looking gobsmacked, especially Josh who didn't know our history, although he certainly knew Brent. Turning back to Claire, I tried to read what she was thinking but she just flashed me a drunken smile before turning around and facing the bakery. None of us quite knew what to say, so we all just stood in silence, watching as Brent returned and trying to pretend that nothing had happened.

The smell inside the small shop was intoxicating, the pastries so fresh they were still warm, despite being nearly two am on Christmas morning. As we said our goodbyes to the others, all bound for the clubs, Claire threw me a wink before pausing to pull Brent down a few inches for a kiss.

'She's just messing with you dude, the girl's a psycho,' Josh explained as I filled him in on the way to the beach.

'I know, but… she was so different in Thailand. If I could get her away from Brent, then maybe she'd be like that again,' I said.

'Dude, she's not going to be any different. Any girl that does what she just did is a basket case pure and simple. Anyway, half an hour ago you were drooling over Isabella, who incidentally seemed to be giving you some vibes back at the house.'

'*Vibes*? What do you mean…' I asked.

'I mean, she was giving you some *vibes* and what's more she's *sane*,' Josh explained.

'Vibes…*right*,' I repeated, hoping he meant good vibes.

The road we were walking along broke off into a car park, which ended at the ocean. I could hear the roar of distant waves coming through the night sky but try as I might, I couldn't see anything. We stood at the car park edge for a minute listening to the crashing surf and feeling the warm salty breeze blowing in from over the water. Josh began mumbling curses to himself about the onshore winds ruining the morning surf. He then took a moment to point out the general direction of the town's surf breaks, although I could see nothing in the dark.

To our left I could see four or five fires dotted along the night horizon, and to our right a black void. Handfuls of people were already descending down to our left, headed for the fires, but as I made a move towards the left, I turned around to see Josh headed in the opposite direction.

'Where are you going? The fires are this way,' I said.

'Yeah they are but our fire is this way,' he replied with certainty.

'There's nothing but darkness that way, surely they will have lit the fire by now,' I argued.

'Probably, but you won't be able to see it from here. If you have a fire out in the open like those ones,' he said pointing down to our left, 'then too many unwanted people will always turn up. So a couple of months ago we found a spot just behind a rock outcrop that's out of view until you get right upon it.'

'Okay, fair enough. Lead the way.'

Walking along the dark beach, with a new moon hidden from sight, the only light came from the distant lighthouse, it's beam providing a little illumination to the beach every few seconds. After fifteen minutes or so, skirting the incoming tide line, we finally caught sight of an orange glow rising up through flickers of smoke.

Ten others from the party were already there, sat around the blazing fire. Josh made a beeline straight for Ambur, who was sat to Isabella's right, while I decided to fill the gap between Steve and Noodle, hoping for an opportunity to ask Steve about borrowing a board. As I sat down, I glanced across the fire towards Isabella and saw she was smiling at me, taking me right back to Newquay when Noodle's girlfriend Fran had done the same. Only this time I hoped there was no hooded villain about to come and steal the beauty away. Passing the doughnuts and pastries out, I saw Isabella mouth what I took to be 'thank you,' before she turned to talk with Josh and Ambur.

'This reminds me of Newquay,' I said, turning to Noodle who was busy lighting up a joint.

'Yeah, I guess there are similarities, but if you live this kind of lifestyle then it becomes common wherever you go,' he replied, blowing out a lungful of smoke and grinning.

'Sounds good to me,' I replied.

'The way I see it, if you're a backpacker then you're either a sheep following the crowd, or you're living your dream and walking your own path. So you need to decide what you are really doing here Matt,' Noodle said.

'Hey, don't knock the sheep, they're my bread and butter,' Steve chipped in.

'Yeah, well they're also bloody annoying,' Noodle said, passing me the joint.

'Some are, not all. Matt, just make sure you have fun, screw what the Noodle says,' Steve laughed.

'Right,' I said, hoping I wasn't a sheep but at the same time unsure how not to be one. 'Steve, Noodle said you might have an old surfboard I could borrow, to learn on,' I said, changing the subject, but then realising I might be sounding like one of the many sheep I knew who came to Byron Bay just to learn to surf.

'He mentioned that to me too. I'll drop a board off to you or Noodle in the morning,' he replied.

As the fire dwindled so did our numbers, until it was just the few of us that had sat around the cushions in the lounge. We had spread out around the glowing embers, pairing off but still keeping the conversation moving around the circle. Josh and Ambur were sat across from Isabella, Steve and I. I couldn't help but wonder if Isabella was giving me *vibes* as we talked. If she was I obviously wasn't tuned in enough, as I couldn't see her being anything but friendly. When Steve got up to leave, Noodle and Lola made a move too, leaving just the just the four of us lying about in the dark night, illuminated like clockwork by the lighthouse, the heat dying in the remains of the fire.

Watching Josh and Ambur cuddle up, I glanced over to Isabella, considering my chances of getting a bit warmer with her but, still sat a couple of feet away, she seemed too distant to be able to make a move on.

Smoking another joint, I could feel that sleep was creeping upon me and I really didn't want to wake up on the beach again. As I got up to my feet to make my excuses and head back, the other three decided to call it a night too, joining me for a stroll back in the dark. Josh and Ambur were wrapped up in each other, catching up on time lost whilst he was in Fiji, leaving Isabella and I to walk together, ahead of them.

'It's a nice night,' I said, awkwardly lost for words, the tide now right up high.

'Yeah, it's been good. Thanks for coming to the party.'

'So are you going surfing tomorrow?' I asked.

'Maybe… are you going to kiss me tonight?' she asked, stopping as I turned, registering what she'd said.

'Maybe…' I replied, moving in close and kissing her. Her lips were like silk and I felt as though I was kissing for the first time ever. The seconds seemingly lasted for hours before she finished with two quick pecks on the lips and a thoughtful smile, as she took my hand and we walked on.

Eight

Maybe the paddock had grown a little, or perhaps the horse was moving just that little bit quicker but for a split second, before Josh began shaking my bunk bed, it galloped. As the two worlds collided, for a brief moment, my mind was lost somewhere between the horse-inhabited paddock of my dreams and the messy dormitory of my reality.

'Dude!' a distinctive disembodied Californian voice called into my ear.

'Urrghh... *what*?' I groaned.

'Do you always snore so loudly?'

'... *What*?'

'Get up, time for your first surf lesson. Got your board right here,' he said, as Josh and a towering surfboard came into focus.

'*Surf*? What time is it?' I asked, peering down from my top bunk.

'Around eight-thirty, time to get up and catch some festive waves my friend.'

'I only just got to bed a couple of hours ago,' I pleaded, turning back over.

'Come on Matt, it'll wake you up,' Isabella's disembodied voice called out.

'*Isabella*?' I asked the room, swiftly finding the energy to sit up and survey the room for her.

'Come on, get up Matt,' Ambur spoke up, as I caught a glimpse of the two girls sat on the vacant bottom bed of an adjacent bunk.

The room was thrown into silence again, as the others left, for the benefit of my disgruntled roommates who'd also been woken. Wiping my eyes, I crawled out of my sleeping bag and fumbled about, putting on my red board shorts before stepping out into the hallway where Isabella and Ambur were both waiting, wearing flowery shorts and bikini tops. Downstairs, Josh and Noodle were looking after the boards, both looking wide awake and raring to go, Noodle was in his baggy green boardshorts, Josh still wearing the grey and red shorts from the night before. Only Lola was missing from the group, but she was, Noodle assured me, already on the beach choosing instead to do a little yoga.

Walking barefoot through the backstreets towards the sea with the others, carrying Steve's huge spare board under my arm, I felt I was cool. To any real surfer, I figured, I must have been instantly recognised as a beginner, but in my mind, I was now as cool as every other wave rider out there.

Arriving at the wreck, I could now see how it had got its name. Jutting out of the water, beyond the breaking waves, a couple of pieces of wood were visible, which were remains of a ship that had run aground. Watching the others wading into the water, heading out to where the waves where breaking at shoulder height, Josh took me aside and showed me the basics on the dry sand. He instructed me to lie down on the sand and pretend to paddle for an imaginary wave, one that neither myself nor the other surfers strolling along the beach and laughing could see. As I paddled for *the wave*, Josh then instructed me to jump up to my feet in one swift motion, a technique I remembered having seen Keanu Reeves perform with just as little grace in Point Break. When Josh had finally grown bored of yelling, laughing and pushing me, he finally suggested we should hit the real waves.

The first wave of my life hit me as I was paddling out, trying desperately to keep up with Josh. It caused me to slide off the side of my board and threw me around under the water. In the distance I could see Noodle catching a wave and effortlessly carving across the face. He rode it right in until he was level with us both, but about twenty feet to our right. With just as much ease he then disappeared, smoothly navigating the incoming waves to find himself back out in the waiting line-up with the others within moments, while I struggled just to pull myself back up onto my board and attempt paddling again.

The water was refreshing, although there was no doubt that being dunked under and swallowing down a mouthful of the warm salty water wasn't really my idea of a good way to spend Christmas morning. However, with every wave that hit my face or pushed me off the board, I felt more determined to make my way out to where Josh was waiting to show me lesson two and actually *catch* a wave.

My arms, shoulders and chest were all aching when I finally reached Josh and we were not even as far out as the real surfers. Not even getting a chance to rest, Josh instructed me to turn the board towards the shore and start paddling. As he barked his instructions, I checked the horizon and couldn't see any impending wave but still did the motions as instructed, after a few seconds of splashing, I sure felt the thing. As the wave came up behind, I felt my speed suddenly increase ten-fold, flinging me towards the shore. In the blink of an eye, the next thing I knew, I was under the water being spun around like a rag doll, with the only indication of the surface coming from my leash, which was strapped around my left ankle connecting me to the board. As the leash tugged at my leg I followed its direction to the surface, another wave broke on my head pushing me back under. Surfacing again, I managed a gulp of air and got a hand on my board before a bigger, third wave came through and sent me back down.

I could hear Josh's laughter before I could see him, discovering he was in the shallows, having caught a wave while I was fighting for breath. Struggling to pull myself back onto the board, I watched as he then effortlessly paddled passed me shouting a few words of encouragement and suggesting I follow him, but it was a few more minutes before I managed to reach him for another attempt.

The second and third waves were pretty much the same as the first; I swallowed some more water and managed to bump my head on my board on the latter attempt. Wave number four was different though, paddling as hard as I could, I felt the familiar lift as the wave caught up with me, but instead of being flung down into the turbulent water I went forwards and clung onto the board for dear life. Bouncing along the ocean surface, feeling the wave's power start to diminish, I realised that I had yet to stand up, so with all of my might I went through the motions practiced on the sand, pushing up and leaping to my feet. As quickly as I was up, I was back in the water, but the ride was enough to leave a huge Cheshire grin on my face.

'Yeeaaah!' Josh shouted as he rode a wave in towards me.

'Did you see that?' I yelled. 'I stood up!' I called back at him, still buzzing from the adrenalin.

'Yeah dude, now there's a Christmas present I bet you've not had before,' Josh replied, as we both started paddling back out.

'Beats mum's roast turkey that's for sure,' I laughed, as a small wave came through and knocked me off the board.

A couple of hours later, walking back to the hostel by a different route, the grin still plastered across my face, I trailed at the back of the group taking the opportunity to walk alongside Isabella. As I tried to approach the subject of the kiss, my gaze flittered between the pavement, where we followed the wet footprints of the others, and Isabella's eyes, which were gleaming in the morning sun and smiling back at me. As I mentally tried to work out the best approach to my question, Isabella spoke first, curious about my first surfing experience. Excited, but embarrassed that I hadn't been as good as some probably were on their first try, my reply was muted and short. As she then shared her own experiences of learning to surf, which involved just as much near drowning as I had just been subjected to, I began to feel more confident about my beginner's aptitude and opened up more to her, going into uninhibited detail about my few moments of wave riding glory.

Upon reaching Liquid Dreams, we discussed the possibility of joining the big lunch party that Steve was throwing for the backpackers, but decided against it, agreeing instead to get together for a stereotypical Aussie barbeque on the beach. As we started heading off in different directions, I stood looking at Isabella still struggling to find the words to express my feelings, but she again saved me from trying by stepping back and saying goodbye to all of us before she turned and headed home.

With some time to kill before we were due to venture down to the beach, I headed out in search of Ryan and Scott. Their hostel was in a smaller building, without such a large open area as Liquid Dreams, but much like they were in Sydney, I found them sat out on the veranda nursing a couple of beers. This time though they both looked exhausted and hung-over.

'*Hey Matt*,' Scott wearily said as he saw me approach. 'Merry Christmas,' he said, weakly holding up his beer in salute.

'Yeah,' Ryan concurred, 'Merry Christmas buddy.'

'And a very Merry Christmas to yourselves chaps,' I replied, a little too loud and energetic for them, as they both looked at me in horror. 'You boys don't appear to be enjoying it so much though,' I said.

'It's not as bad it looks… Another beer in the system and I'll be good enough to walk,' Ryan said weakly, trying a smile.

'Excellent, so how was last night?' I asked.

'Obviously a later one than yours, how can you have so much energy?' Scott asked.

'Not sure, especially as I was up early for a surf. Did you at least manage to pull?'

'No, I wish,' Ryan said, his voice croaky. 'But tell me, what the hell possessed you to get up early on Christmas Day and go for a surf? You're crazier than I thought.'

'I didn't get much choice to be honest, but I'm glad I did. And you won't believe it, but I pulled last night,' I said, glad to have someone to brag to about Isabella.

'Well, yeah, we know. We saw you remember. You don't have to rub it in,' Scott grumbled.

'You saw me?' I asked, puzzled for a moment. 'How...? Oh wait, you mean Claire? *No*, I'm talking about Isabella,' I said, remembering Claire's kiss.

'*Isabella*?' Ryan and Scott said in unison.

'That's right, which reminds me, we're all having a barbie down the beach in a little while if you feel up to it,' I said.

'Is Isabella going to be there?' Scott asked.

'Definitely,'

'Great, well assuming my head stops banging, I'm in,' Ryan replied, before raising the beer to his lips.

The Canadians were nearly thirty minutes late when they finally turned up at Liquid Dreams, both wearing Santa hats. Noodle and the others had gone on ahead, but as we went to leave Brent came out of the kitchen and called after us. For a moment I froze up, thinking he'd found out about the kiss, or worse - Thailand. However, as he got closer his face cracked into a smile. 'What are you all doing today?' he asked.

'Ah... just heading down to the beach,' Ryan croaked, without enthusiasm.

'You're not sticking around for the hostel party?'

'No, we're having a barbie on the beach,' Scott said, before receiving a dirty look from Ryan.

'If you and Claire want to come, we're going now,' I reluctantly offered, feeling obliged to ask, on account of it being Christmas, but hoping he and Claire were staying at the hostel party.

'Really? Okay, hang on I'll just ask Claire, but I reckon she'd be keen, a *barbie on the beach*,' Brent said, with an imitated Aussie twang. 'Sounds like a proper Aussie way to spend Christmas Day, you know.'

'*Why* did you just invite him?' Ryan asked me as Brent disappeared in search of Claire. 'I'd have thought you of all people would be wanting to avoid him and *her*.'

'Well, you know, it's Christmas and I know what it's like not knowing many people and needing a friend or two. Claire won't want to go if she knows I'm going though, so don't worry,' I replied.

'Seems to me like you're still hoping there's a chance that Claire's going to ditch him for you,' Scott said.

'Not until he nails Isabella for number three, though,' Ryan smiled.

'No and no to both those comments,' I said in a hush, as Brent and Claire came into view.

It took us nearly an hour to find the others, not realising that they wouldn't be on the sand itself but on the grassy banks, at a shaded public barbeque. Fortunately for us, they'd only just started cooking after waiting for a family before us to finish. Introducing the Canadians, Brent and Claire to the others, I was glad Isabella and Ambur didn't know anything about Claire, especially as Ryan's earlier comment had started me thinking on the walk down about how good it would be to win Ben's challenge with Isabella. However, as I watched Isabella and Claire chatting and giggling together I began to regret inviting her and Brent along. I was not only paranoid at what Claire was telling Isabella but finding it impossible to get away from Brent.

The barbeque tasted great, washed down with the first beers of the day, but as we moved down onto the sand and into the hot sun I felt like I needed to either swim or sleep, as the fatigue of the last couple of days began to seep in, forcing the occasional yawn to the surface. However, finding a willing sidekick for the swim was surprisingly difficult, nobody else fancied exercising with their full stomachs. Nobody except for Claire, that is. She didn't volunteer at first, but when it became clear that no one else was keen she happily followed me into the water.

'So, you *didn't* get arrested on Koh Pha Ngan then?' I asked as soon as we were out of earshot.

'*Arrested*? Is that what you think happened to me?' she asked.

'Well, from my perspective, I came back to the room, the lock was broken, you were gone, your bags were gone. I figured you'd been arrested because of the drugs.'

'*What drugs*?' she asked. 'You mean the *diet pills*? They really did bugger all and no one was going to bother arresting me for that. They're legal, just hard to get on the island at that time cause everyone's buying them,' she explained.

'Right, silly me. So, let me get this straight, you left because Brent turned up.'

'Yes,' she said, as we entered the water.

'And you didn't break the door?'

'No, it was already like that.'

'Was my bag there? I mean when you came back?' I asked.

'Your bag? Yeah, I think so,' she replied.

'Then what the hell happened to it?' I asked but it was too late, Claire was already diving into the small incoming waves, signalling our conversation was over. I stood watching her swim out for a moment and then slowly followed, knowing I could be being watched from the beach.

A few minutes later, ducking under an incoming wave, I felt something strike my ankle. As I screamed underwater, I swallowed a mouthful of salty water, whatever it was had me in a firm grip for a moment before letting go as I made it to the surface.

'What the hell...?' I yelped before seeing Claire pop up beside me.

'*Bitch,*' I mumbled as she started laughing.

'Sorry Matt,' she giggled. 'I'm just having some fun,' she said, reaching for my groin underwater.

'Fun?' I blurted as I tried to swim backwards away from her reach. 'If you want fun, go have it with Brent, not me. He's your boyfriend remember?' I said.

'Oh, come on, what he doesn't know won't hurt him. I thought we were having fun in Thailand,' she said, making another attempt to grab at my crotch.

'We were, I think. But I'm not going to be your bit on the side because if he does find out it may not hurt him as much as he'll hurt me,' I said, turning to swim back in, leaving Claire playing in the waves.

Back on the beach, I was fuming but trying not to show it, as I sat down as far from Brent as I could, grabbed a beer and sat in silence watching the crowded afternoon surf. A few minutes later Claire returned, announcing that she had a headache and was going back to the hostel for a lie down. If anyone suspected our change in attitudes had been affected by the swim, then they didn't show it.

Not long after, we lost the Canadians to their hangovers, determined to get a few hours of sleep before hitting the clubs and beer again in the evening. For the rest of us, the afternoon was spent relaxing on the beach, dozing and enjoying another swim, which turned into a bodysurf competition as Noodle and Josh showed me how to catch waves without a board.

As the hours wore on, we decided to move the party back to Isabella's house, where we kept drinking and smoking into the evening. The perfect end to a perfect Christmas Day, that was until Isabella noticed a missed message on her phone.

'Ah, *sweet...*' she said to herself, listening to the message, before realising we were all watching her. 'My little niece, it is her fifth birthday today, I sent her a present and she called up to say thank you and wish me a happy Christmas. She's so cute.'

'*Shit...*' I mumbled, as I listened to Isabella.

'What?' she asked, sat leaning against my side but still I hadn't had another kiss or an opportunity to try.

'I forgot to phone my parents and wish them a happy Christmas. Oh man... I'm like the world's worst son,' I groaned.

'Relax Matt, England is something like twelve hours behind, so technically it'll still be Christmas there when it's tomorrow morning here, so just phone them tomorrow,' Lola explained.

'Is that what you're doing then?' I asked her.

'No, I phoned my mum earlier,' she said

'And me,' Isabella smiled.

'Oh shit, maybe I should phone now,' I said, not relishing the thought of going back to the hostel to find my phone.'

'I haven't called mine yet dude,' Josh slurred.

'*Really*? Okay well maybe I'll wait until tomorrow as well.'

'But... that's just because it's not Christmas there until tomorrow, Cali is something like twenty hours behind here,' he smiled to himself.

'What about you Noodle?' I asked, hoping for another Brit to be as slack.

'I haven't got any family to call, but I texted my old mates in London earlier,' Noodle said.

'*Shit*, I really am a bad son,' I said. 'Right, I'm going to get up and call them now.'

Isabella had decided to tag along and get some fresh air, taking the Santa hat she'd stolen from one of the Canadians and putting it snugly on over my curly locks. We could hear the hostel party from a couple of streets away still going from lunch time, but thankfully my room was empty as we sat on my bed to make the call.

My phone already had seven missed calls from home, so as I waited for someone to pick up I knew I was going to get an earful. The problem was I felt a little too intoxicated to really care, and as I listened to my panicking mum I had to fight the urge to break into a fit of stoned laughter, especially as Isabella kept pulling faces to make me laugh.

118

Ten minutes later, I hung up, pleased that I'd made the effort to call on Christmas Day and even more chuffed that I wasn't there, going through the same old motions for another year. It was in that moment that Isabella chose to bestow her Christmas present on me, leaning in for a kiss, which caused me to smile and as our lips pressed the smile grew into a snigger, just moments before a mutual fit of hysterics ensued.

Nine

Slowly coming out of my slumber, I was surprised to be waking up in Isabella's lounge still fully clothed and with a Santa hat on my head. Hazy early morning light filtered in through a gap in the curtains and Isabella, the source of my disturbance, walked in from the kitchen, dressed in her white surf shorts and a maroon bikini top.

'Morning,' I croaked to Isabella.

'Morning dude,' Josh said, poking his head around the corner from the kitchen.

'Buenos días, Matt, are you going to come surfing?' Isabella asked, whilst I was still trying to piece together how I was lying fully clothed in her lounge when her and Josh were already up and preparing to surf.

'It can't be time for a surf already, I don't even remember going to bed,' I groaned.

'You didn't, you passed out after we got back. You looked so peaceful I decided not to disturb you,' Isabella said.

Twenty minutes later we were back at the wreck. On our way to the beach we stopped off at Liquid Dreams to pick up Steve's old board and find Noodle, but neither he nor Steve were around, already, we suspected, in the water. As we scanned the horizon looking at the tiny waves coming through, we could see that Noodle wasn't out already, because the surf was empty.

After a couple of minutes spent watching the sea, Josh seemed certain that we could still catch a few of the tiny rollers that were intermittently coming through, and so Isabella and I, assuming he knew, best followed him out. This time there were neither beachside instructions nor any waves throwing me about and under, but still I watched in frustration as Josh and Isabella made it all seem so easy to catch and ride the tiny waves. After lots of paddling about whilst watching the others fly past, my first wave of the day was a messy affair as I momentarily perched on one leg before toppling straight over. My second and final wave of the day wasn't much better as I wasted the majority of it lying down on the board, trying to summon the energy to pop up onto my feet. By the time I did make it, the wave had lost its power and the board just sank under my weight, acting as deflated as I felt.

Only half an hour after first paddling out we were back on the sand, having given up trying to get good rides out in the small surf.

'How were your waves?' Josh asked me, as we advanced up the beach.

'Not great. I thought smaller waves would have been easier, but I caught more yesterday,' I said, feeling rather defeated.

'You need a better board, that beaten up old plank's not great for learning on. A better board will give you a better experience,' he said.

'You'll also find that the more you give to the ocean, the more it'll give back to you,' Isabella sagely remarked. 'I almost gave up surfing after my first few times as I was just ending up frustrated and half drowned by it all. After a bit, the surfing gets more rewarding though and then there's no looking back,' she said.

'But,' Josh said, 'you should buy a board, that way you can get used to riding the same board every time you surf. If you want me to, I can go with you and help you pick out a good one?' Josh volunteered.

'Yeah, maybe,' I answered, before remembering the surfboard for sale on the hostel notice board. 'What sort of size board do you think I should get?' interested to hear Josh's thoughts.

'It's tricky I guess, you'll need something big and buoyant but not too big as you need to be able to travel with it. Unless of course you don't intend leaving Byron, in which case get a long board,' he said, which largely echoed Noodle's opinion.

'Well, I guess I've got a few days to think about it anyhow, what with the waves being virtually non-existent,' I said.

'It'll be bigger tomorrow,' Isabella said.

'How do you know that, is it something to do with the moon?' I asked.

'Not really, there's a big low pressure out towards Fiji at the moment. Should be bringing a big swell in a day or two. It'll definitely have picked up by tomorrow morning,' Josh said.

'So we should have just waited for tomorrow, rather than trying to catch teeny waves today then,' I said.

'We could have, but it's always worth getting wet and besides, it's good to be able to surf all conditions and sizes, it'll make you better for when the surf is really good,' Josh explained.

Returning to the hostel, I dropped off the board and decided to head out and explore the town, thinking about Josh's surf prediction. The past few days, I'd been noticing that I was the only one who seemed to have problems walking barefoot to the beach and back, as stones dug into my soft soles yet these didn't appear to bother anyone else. So in an effort to toughen up, I decided to forego the flip-flops, feeling the warm concrete as I eagerly headed into town.

The town centre looked very different in the bright daylight. The only place I recognised was the bakery, which was open but void of customers. Along the main street almost every building was a surf shop or organic café, one of which I knew was Ambur's although I had no idea which one. The population, at first glance, could have been split into three distinct groups of surfers, hippies and backpackers, although the line between each was definitely blurred and some would have surely fit into all three categories.

After walking into a couple of surf shops and eyeing up their racks of bright white boards, in varying shapes and sizes, I realised that I had absolutely no idea what I was looking for and began to understand why both Noodle and Josh had offered their expertise in helping me pick one.

Deciding to put off looking until I was with one of the others, I headed for an internet café to see if I had any news from home. It had been a few days since I'd last checked my emails and I was hoping for more news than I had had. Trawling through the junk, I found one from Rachel, another from Kermit and for the first time, one from Ben. Opening Ben's email first, my smile was lost as I saw it was just an electronic Christmas card, with a short message saying – *Not sure I completely believe you managed to bed two women, especially without any photographic evidence. Less than a week left to go mate, will you be a legend or a loser? Merry Christmas   Ben*
There was nothing about home, nothing to tell me what he'd been up to during the past few weeks. There was just a reminder about the challenge, which although I'd more or less given up on, I began to once again think about just how good it would be to return home a legend, rather than the loser, which was how I was beginning to think of Ben.

The emails from Kermit and Rachel were again short and snappy, both wishing me a good Christmas and neglecting to mention what was going on in their lives. It was becoming clear that despite my lengthy emails telling them all about my adventures, they didn't seem to realise that I needed something similar in return.

The rest of the afternoon went by pretty quickly. I visited the Canadians' hostel and ended up playing cards into the evening. I was introduced to Chris, a sinewy blond Norwegian with a bushy beard, who worked at the hostel and joined in for a few rounds. It was obvious from our conversation that the Canadians had told Chris about my bet to bed three women and the pitfalls I'd been struggling against.

Calling time on the evening, after what felt like endless rounds of *shithead* and beers, I staggered back to Liquid Dreams around ten o'clock, desperate for a decent night's sleep, my mind whirling at just how good it would be to accomplish the challenge and become a legend, not only back home, but with the Canadians and anyone else who cared to know.

The morning of the twenty-seventh was lost in sleep. There were no wake up calls and I had slept through any of the noise my roommates made. When I did finally surface, Steve was eating lunch on the veranda.

'G'day Matt, you only just woken up?' he asked.

'Yeah, but I think I needed the sleep. I guess there was no surf this morning, huh?' I asked, thinking that I would have been woken if there had been.

'There was, yeah. It's pretty good out there, the swell's picked up. Tomorrow should be better if the wind keeps away,' he said, leaving me wondering why nobody had bothered to get me.

'You haven't seen Noodle or Josh around have you?' I asked, thinking that maybe they too had missed the morning surf.

'They were still in the water when I headed back, you could try the Treehouse,' he said.

'The Treehouse?'

'Yeah, it's Ambur's café on Jonson Street,' he said, as I turned and headed off, hoping that if Josh or Noodle were already in town they might have a few spare moments to help me buy a board.

The interior of the Treehouse seemed to be half café and half rainforest, with thriving green plants on the tables and hanging down from the rafters. Behind the counter I could see Ambur occupied with a customer's order, and much to my surprise, beside her was Chris from the Canadians' hostel, working at the café too. Immediately I got a bad feeling about being in the café, remembering that Chris knew something about me that I really didn't want Ambur knowing. As I turned to tiptoe away, I heard my name being called, although not by Chris or Ambur but by Lola who'd spotted me through the jungle. I had no choice but to walk over and join her, trying hard not to look at Chris or Ambur and hoping to sneak past without their noticing.

123

'Hi Lola, what are you doing hiding in the bushes?' I asked, sitting down in the most camouflaged seat at the table.

'I just had a smoothie with Ambur. We've been up doing yoga together the past couple of mornings while you and the others have been surfing,' she said.

'Cool... So is Noodle still surfing?' I asked.

'I think so, didn't you go with him?'

'No, not today but I was hoping he might be around later to help me shop for a board,' I said.

'He might be. Truth is I haven't seen much of him the past couple of days, I think he's having a hard time being back here again,' Lola said, her eyes telling me more about her frustration than her words.

'At least he's got plenty of friends here,' I said. 'I thought he was doing okay.'

'Well, I've hardly seen him, he spent all of yesterday getting wasted with some old mates as there was no surf. Now there is surf, he's spent the whole morning in the water,' she said.

'Maybe it'll be better once you get to New Zealand,' I replied, lost for something cheerful to say.

'If we get that far. Anyway, aren't you going to get something to eat or drink? I assume that's why you're here,' she said, forcing a smile, as I pondered the risk of getting up and going to the counter but was left with little choice.

As Ambur took my order and offered to bring it over, it was clear that Chris hadn't told her about our conversations the night before. So, beginning to relax whilst hoping that he probably either wouldn't recognise or remember me, I headed back to Lola's table, wishing I could stop my imagination running away all the time.

Saying goodbye to Ambur as I left the café with Lola a couple of hours later, ahead of us we spotted Josh and Isabella coming out of a shop together. Instantly my stomach tightened and a wave of jealousy washed over me. This, I told myself, was why they hadn't woken me up, they wanted to spend time together without me around. As we watched them get closer, I wanted to spy on them, to establish if my suspicions were just. Lola, on the other hand, had no idea of the thoughts running through my head and called out to them.

They seemed surprised, but happy, to see us both, Isabella passionately kissing me on the lips as we said hello, sweeping away any doubts I had about our relationship.

'Well, this is a lucky coincidence, Matt was just about to look for you Josh,' Lola said.

'Oh yeah?' Josh said.

'I was?' I asked.

'Something about helping you shop for a surfboard?' she reminded me.

'*Oh yeah*,' I said, breaking through the temporary amnesia brought on by Isabella's kiss and my thoughts of asking her out to dinner. 'I was thinking about what you said yesterday about buying a surfboard and was hoping you might still be keen to help me choose a board.'

'Okay, sure, I can do it now if you like?' Josh said.

'Sounds good… assuming I'm not ruining your plans?' I checked, as I glanced across at Isabella.

'No, don't worry. Issi was just looking for a new book to read and I thought I'd tag along.'

'Shopping for a surfboard is much more exciting though,' Isabella said, 'I reckon you should try the place on the corner first,' she added, pointing down the street, as we all set off in that direction.

Isabella's suggestion only housed a small selection of boards, each of them with interesting artwork and looking great to my untrained eyes, only to be instantly dismissed by both Isabella and Josh. The next shop, Josh's suggestion, had a wider range and he began pulling out a few big boards to inspect them. As I watched him check each one over, I still couldn't understand what he was looking for, but I could see the price tags were almost double the amount I'd hoped to spend.

As soon as I expressed my budget concerns, he put the new board back and led me to another area of less spectacular looking boards, all of which were second hand and in varying states of wear and tear. As he pulled out a couple of yellowish boards, he explained the plusses and minuses of each board before putting it back, still not content with what was available, whilst Isabella and Lola watched and listened.

Just as we were leaving, Josh spotted a board on the racks outside the shop and led me over. As he pulled the board out I could see it looked a little bigger than Steve's old one and in a better condition, although there were still a few noticeable dents. There was no fancy artwork on this board just the word *MinTinTar*, the meaning of which, neither Josh nor the young mop headed shop assistant could explain.

As Josh handed the board over for me to inspect it, he could have been giving me an ironing board, for I had no real understanding about what I was meant to be looking at or for. It looked in good enough condition and the price was reasonable enough, so with Josh's assurance that it would be a good beginner board I handed my hard earned cash over. Momentarily thinking back to the warehouse where I'd earned it, I was pleased that I was using the money as I'd daydreamed about during those endless monotonous hours.

'Now I just need to go surfing,' I said, as we left the shop.

'There's plenty of swell if you fancy a surf this afternoon?' Josh asked.

'Sounds good,' I replied. 'Did you have a surf this morning?' I asked, trying to subtly find out why I hadn't been woken up.

'Yeah, I tried to find you but I don't think you were around. No one answered when I knocked on your door and I couldn't see Noodle or Steve about, so we figured you'd gone for a surf with them already.'

'Shit *really*? I didn't wake up until gone noon, I guess I must have been in a deep sleep when you knocked,' I said. 'But do you fancy a surf now?'

'Definitely, although maybe we should head over to Tallow, the main beach will be pretty crowded right now,' Josh suggested, referring to the beach at the other side of the headland, beyond the towering lighthouse.

Tallow beach had a wild remote feeling, a long stretch of white sand, bordered by lush green trees and wild grass. From the safety of the beach the sea seemed to mirror the rugged surroundings, looking less friendly than the main Byron Bay breaks. Perhaps that was one reason why the crowd in the surf was sparser than I'd expected.

Pulling myself up onto my new surfboard for my first attempt at paddling it, I immediately slid off the side and plunged straight back into the water. My second attempt scored a little more success paddling a few meters until a few small waves crossed my path and pushed me off again. By this time I could already see Josh catching his first wave of the afternoon, just moments before another wall of water pushed me back under. After an eternity, I finally caught up with Josh and Isabella, knackered, but ready to catch my first waves on MinTinTar. But as I waited, bottling out on a couple of waves, I watched as the other two took off on rides, leaving me alone out back, studying the horizon for an easy looking peak.

126

As I saw one that looked like it might be suitable, I turned my board around and began furiously paddling, glancing over my shoulder to check my positioning only to catch sight of two large dorsal fins moving through the water only about ten-feet away. In a brown-shorts moment, I stopped paddling, lifting my arms and legs up as high as I could, whilst still lying on my belly. My gaze fixed on the sharks, I hadn't even noticed that the wave was still creeping up until it was too late. Suddenly a five-foot wall of water crashed down upon me, ripping the board out from underneath me, thrusting me beneath the surface and into a spin.

Eyes wide open under the water, I span around desperately trying to see an attacker, thinking that if I could get a punch in first it might be enough to keep me alive. But as I waited, I felt a yanking at my ankle as the leash tugged me backwards. MinTinTar, on the other end, was caught up in another wave and was taking me with it. As I reluctantly flew backwards, my lungs starting to ache, I gave up on the punching idea and opted to get on the board and out of the water as soon as I possibly could. Gasping for air as I struggled to climb back on, I could see Isabella to my left and tried to warn her, only to find my vocal cords paralyzed by fear.

'Oh look, dolphins!' she said excitedly, pointing behind me.

'*Dolphins*?' I blurted. 'They're not dolphins they're sharks, we need to get out!' I shouted at her.

'*Sharks*? Where? Are you sure?' she asked, before a dorsal fin surfaced between us.

'There! *Shit*!' I yelped, before splashing my way towards the shore.

'Matt! Calm down that's just a dolphin,' Isabella said, stretching a hand out towards it. 'Look at how the fin moves. *Jesus*,' she said, her gaze now appearing to question my sanity.

'Are you sure?'

'Yes, I've often surfed with them here,' Isabella reassured.

'Okay, sorry,' I apologised, as I turned my board back around.

'Trust me next time, okay?'

'Do… Do you fancy having dinner with me tonight?' I asked, feeling it was almost a now or never question that might also help break the tension, although I was slightly concerned that my panicking had dramatically cut her opinion of me.

'Okay, but only if you catch a couple of waves, otherwise we're off,' she joked, as we paddled back out together, my eyes still scanning the water for real sharks.

The euphoria from the surf at Tallow was still buzzing about my head that night as I headed over to Isabella's, only to find the lights off and the house empty. Looking through the windows, I could see no sign of life inside. Perplexed by her absence, I wandered back to Liquid Dreams, thinking that maybe there had been some confusion regarding where we were meant to be meeting.

Back at the hostel, there was no sign of her either. So feeling at a loss, I wandered into town, thinking maybe she would be at the Treehouse café. That too was locked and empty, so I doubled back to the hostel and sat out on the veranda waiting. An hour went by, watching rain turn from a light pitter-patter into a torrential downpour, hammering on the corrugated iron roof above the veranda. Listening to the rain come down, I decided to wander back to Isabella's house to check if she had returned.

Walking barefoot through the warm downpour my t-shirt was clinging to my skin, my shorts soaked. On my return to the small bungalow, I could see a light was now on and after I knocked on the door, I was surprised to see Ambur answering it, opening the door just enough to wedge her scowling head through.

'Hi Ambur, is Isabella in?' I asked, as water trickled off my chin.

'She doesn't want to see you mate, *bye*,' Ambur said, as she moved her head back and went to close the door. Jamming my foot in and shouldering my weight against her own, I managed to leave a small gap.

'Why not? I was here at eight, I didn't stand her up,' I pleaded.

'No, *you're right, you didn't*, but we found out about your little bet and we know you were just trying to get her into bed, so I think you should just go,' she said, pushing the door again with enough force to close it shut.

'*Fuck!*' I yelled, about to pound on the door but managing to stop myself. 'Isabella, please it isn't like that! Let me explain please. Yes, I did make a stupid bet with friends back home but I never intended to try and win it!' I shouted into the door, before being taken by surprise as it reopened.

'Isabella,' I said, trying not to smile as I saw her in the doorway.

'Matt, please don't. I know you were bragging about it last night, so you're obviously still doing it. Just show me a little respect and leave me alone,' she said, closing the door before I could get a word in.

Stepping through the muddy puddles in Isabella's garden and shutting the small gate behind me, I felt nauseous. I couldn't believe that I'd messed everything up with Isabella, just when I thought things were starting to go my way. The last thing I wanted to do was go back to Liquid Dreams and be sociable, so I headed out in the opposite direction away from the town centre. I passed through quiet residential streets, not seeing another sole, the rain blinding me at times as I slowly weaved my way towards the beach.

As I stood on the wet sand, I noticed that the predicted big swell had arrived. Although I couldn't see much in the dark night, other than white lines of broken water pushing forwards into the shallows, I could hear the roar of the surf, booming as each wave broke.

For a brief moment I contemplated going for a swim as I had done during the storm on Koh Phi Phi, but an inner voice was keeping me firmly on the sand, telling me that this was a very different ball game in the dark and with big waves. So I just sat down on the wet sand and listened to the ocean crashing, trying desperately to think of how I could repair the damage with Isabella.

I stayed on the beach until I was shivering, reluctant to go back. I sat watching, listening and thinking. I wanted to blame the Canadians for the mess I was in, as I knew it must have been Chris who'd let slip to Ambur, but I knew deep down it was pointless to point the finger at anyone but myself. I had been bragging and joking about the bet and I knew from Isabella's perspective she had every reason to hate me. I only hoped her contempt wasn't contagious.

The following morning I woke up early, keen for a surf, but knowing it was highly unlikely that either Josh or Noodle would bother waking me. Josh, because I knew he'd have gone to Isabella's first, and Noodle because he'd been off the radar for the past couple of days. So, grabbing my new board, I headed out to the beach, excitedly nervous at the prospect of trying to surf the bigger waves I knew had arrived.

The closer I got to the beach, the stronger the wind became, blowing in across the ocean. As I took my first glimpse at the rough and violent seas I felt the spray blowing up and into my face leaving a salty taste on my lips. There were no surfers or swimmers out in the water, no doubt put off by the choppy grey water and the early morning hour. As I stood on the cold sand, tightly grasping my board to stop it being blown away, I contemplated going back to the hostel and back to bed, before Josh's advice about needing to surf in all conditions popped into my head and pushed me forwards.

Standing in the shallow warm water I decided that I wouldn't go out far, just enough to catch a few small waves, but not right out to the back where better surfers would have normally headed. As I charged into the roaring surf, I wasn't even sure I'd get that far as the strong waves and currents constantly threw me around and back towards the beach.

Persevering through the choppy white water, I found that no matter how hard I paddled I just couldn't reach the breaking waves, since the current was holding me back. Until, in what seemed like a blink of the eye, I was thrust into the swirling heart of the incoming waves, as they peaked up and slammed down into the angry ocean below. Suddenly feeling intimidated by the raw power all around, I realised I was in way over my head and decided to catch a wave into the beach and call it a day. I didn't have to wait long as right in front of me a towering wave jacked up from out of nowhere. Swinging my board around towards the shore and paddling with all my might, I felt the wave lifting me up, holding me for a split second as I looked down to the ocean's surface a good twelve-feet below me, hands gripping the side of the board ready to spring to my feet before I realised all too late that I was being thrown straight down instead of forwards.

As I fell through the air I remained lying face down on my board, clinging on for dear life, before slapping the water and bouncing for the briefest moment, just as a twelve-foot wall of water crashed down on my head. Instantly, my board was ripped from my grasp as I was pushed down deep, the pressure causing a sharp pain in my left ear, the force of the water ripping my ankle leash off, separating me from my surfboard lifeline. Trying to swim up to the surface, I struck sand. Scrambling around to change direction, the pressure in my ear eased slightly as I surfaced and sucked in a lungful of oxygen before being hammered under again by another wave.

Breaking through the surface again, through blurry, stinging eyes I looked up expecting to see another wave crashing down, but there was nothing. Glancing around, my surfboard was nowhere to be seen and the beach looked further away than I'd remembered. I still couldn't see any other surfers out but there were three people walking along the beach, one of whom seemed to have decided to run in for a swim, which gave me a confidence boost that I wasn't the only mad one.

Treading water, I decided my best bet would be to body surf a wave in, as I'd learnt to do on Christmas Day, but the ocean had mellowed out with only small powerless bits of chop coming through. With not enough to catch, I began stroking my way back in towards the shore, hoping to catch something on the way.

As I continued to swim in, the land didn't appear to be getting any nearer but the swimmer did. As I kept on powering through, the guy got even closer before I realised it was Noodle.

'Hey Noodle, you really like your swims in stormy water huh?' I called out as soon as he was in earshot.

'Matt! What the *fuck* are you doing out here?' He shouted, his voice livid.

'I was surfing, but my leash came off, I'm now just trying to swim in,' I replied.

'Committing suicide more like. Didn't you see the red flags?'

'*Yeah...* why?' I asked.

'*What?* ... Red flags mean the water is too dangerous to go in anywhere. Haven't you noticed how far you're drifting?' Glancing over his shoulder I felt my heart miss a beat as I noticed not so much how far away we were from the coast but rather how far away I was from the wreck, where I'd first paddled out. I couldn't even see it.

'Oh *shit!*' I yelled, starting to swim in. 'Lets go then,' I called out peering over my shoulder only to find that Noodle wasn't swimming and despite my efforts I wasn't putting any distance between us.

'Matt! Stop!' he yelled. 'You'll drown going that way! Follow me!'

The route Noodle chose back to the shore seemed to be an illogical one especially as my limbs were beginning to ache. Instead of heading straight into the beach as I'd tried to do, Noodle took us diagonally towards the lighthouse. After a few minutes I could see we were making progress but it felt as though we were still just moving parallel to the coast. As fatigue began to set in, I switched from crawl to breaststroke and back again, trying my best to keep up with Noodle through the rough water, wondering for a moment if a dolphin might pop up and offer us a lift back in.

After what felt like at least half an hour, we found ourselves surrounded by breaking waves again. Pausing for the first time, Noodle turned back to face me, looking calm and relaxed despite our hard swim, but as I kept going to catch up with him I realised he was looking past me. Glancing back to see a wave tottering over behind my head, threatening to break right on top of me, I instinctively swam back out, diving under the breaking face to avoid being pummelled. As soon I surfaced, I swam back in, meeting Noodle still treading water before he silently turned back towards the beach and carried on swimming, pausing every few strokes to check back at the breaking waves. Another few minutes of following this pattern and diving under a few passing monsters, Noodle suddenly yelled instructions to swim, as though I hadn't been doing that before. A glance over my shoulder, told me what he had in mind, seeing a big hump beginning to jack up. As I moved my heavy arms as fast as I could through the choppy water, I was astonished to see Noodle step up into a new gear, as though he really hadn't been trying until now. As I felt the roller pass underneath me, I could see Noodle flying forwards and disappearing in the crash of the wave.

Waiting for Noodle to surface, I realised that I could now see a small group on the beach, one of which seemed to be holding my surfboard. In fact, as I kept stroking forwards, I realised I knew them all. I could clearly see Josh taking his shirt off only to be held back from entering the water by Lola, Isabella and Ambur. As I tried to ascertain what was going on and where Noodle had gone, I turned to see another big wave quickly approaching. The two options of either diving under it or risking being thrown down and under rushed through my weary mind and without Noodle nearby, I felt a twinge of fear and dread rush over me. In what seemed like slow motion I could see Josh breaking free from the girls and running in before being stopped by Noodle who had emerged from the shallows and was looking in my direction. Knowing he was alright, I realised I needed to catch this wave if I was ever going to get my aching, heavy legs back onto the sand. So through burning pain in my shoulders, my arms started to drag me forwards to catch the peak lurking behind me.

As I felt a wave go by beneath me, I wanted to scream, my energy was almost all spent but still I kept going, suddenly being lifted up and catapulted across the curving face of the following wave. Stiffening my body like a rigid board, I tried to keep my eyes open as I bounced around the surface, keeping on it until I was only about four metres away from the shore. As my ride finished I tried to put my feet down to walk in but as my body sank under the water, the sand was still out of depth. The next thing I knew, Josh had grabbed me and was pulling me in until I touched down on terra firma and lay out exhausted.

'Are you okay dude?' Josh asked with concern, as he wrung out the water from his shorts. Nodding, I felt humiliated that I had needed to be saved.

'What the hell were you doing out there?' Isabella coldly asked as she sat beside Noodle and looked closely at his shoulder, which I could see had a few lines of blood running down.

'Surfing,' I answered.

'*Surfing?*' she exclaimed. '*What the hell is wrong with you?*'

As I moved my mouth to answer, I decided to resist arguing with her any further, undoubtedly I figured it would have all come back to my bet. So in an effort to leave things in the mess they were already in, I summoned all the energy I had left, slowly rose to my feet, picked up my surfboard, and thanked Noodle before trudging back up the beach towards the hostel. As I moved away I could hear Lola shouting after me but I couldn't turn around, to do so would have exposed my tears of quiet despair.

Back at the hostel, I lay in my bed, mentally and physically exhausted. I felt at a complete loss, I knew the town was now closed to anyone wanting to get in or out, so I was stuck in Byron Bay, but I also knew I wouldn't be able to spend my time with Isabella and the others again. I couldn't even face the prospect of seeing any of them after such a humiliating past few hours. As though that wasn't bad enough, I also had Claire trying her best to get me killed by her psychotic boyfriend. The only friends I knew I had left were the Canadians, which was fine, except all they ever seemed to do was drink beer and play cards.

After a couple of lonely hours of contemplation and digesting my guidebook on ideas of where to go next, Noodle came to see me. At first I ignored his knocking, but just when I thought he'd gone, one of my roommates returned, letting him in. As he walked in, I couldn't help but feel ashamed looking like a sulking child, sat on my top bunk, hiding away from my parents.

'Hey Matt, how you feeling?' he asked, as he approached my bunk.

'Knackered... you?' I replied. Trying to look indifferent by what had happened earlier.

'My shoulder's pretty sore, where I got slammed into the sand but it'll be fine. *You alright though?*' he asked again.

'*Yeah*, just wounded pride, really,' I honestly replied.

'You ever seen Big Wednesday, Matt?' he asked, as he picked up my surfboard, looking over it.

'*What*, the surf movie?'

'That's the one,' he replied, his gaze still on the board.

'Sure, it's a classic,' I said, thinking about all the times I'd watched it when I was meant to have been revising.

'Well, there's a scene in that where coincidently the main guy Matt, is screwed up, has lost his friends, hit the bottle, and doesn't know where to turn next.'

'Yeah, I know it, he causes a car crash,' I said, sitting up and paying attention as I watched him continue to study my board, still not looking at me.

'That's right,' he agreed, 'and after the car crash Matt goes to see the old surfboard shaper called Bear, and tells him what happened and how he's screwed up.'

'I remember,' I replied, not sure quite what Noodle was trying to get at.

'Well, Bear tells Matt that you need a friend when you're wrong and when you're right you don't need nothing,' he said, pausing and looking up from the board for the first time, meeting my eyes. 'I told you before that I nearly died surfing in Indo, what I didn't tell you is that it wasn't my mate Guerrero's actions in the water that saved my life. Although he did save me on a particular occasion, I could have easily gone back in the water at a later time when he wasn't around. What saved me was that Guerrero reminded me that I still had friends who cared. I blamed myself for Fran's death and I'd turned away from my friends thinking they blamed me too. I keep forgetting this fact at times, but I'm trying hard to get over what happened and let others in,' he said, pausing. 'I don't know what you thought you were trying to prove by walking away from us all earlier but we are your friends. *Yes*, Isabella's a little upset with you but she'll get over it. I know you were in a pretty lonely place before I met you in Koh Phi Phi, as was I, and neither of us really need to go back there mate.'

'Really? So you're not all pissed off with me and think I'm a loser?' I asked, letting Noodle's words soak in and energise me.

'Not all of us,' he smiled. 'Something Steve once told me was that if you don't pay attention when throwing a boomerang, it might just come back and hit you on the head,' he smiled, 'and the best cure for a boomerang to the head is a cold beer or two.'

'Yeah, why not,' I said, lowering myself off the top bunk.

'Well, at least for both our sakes the year's nearly over, fresh starts all round, I reckon,' Noodle said, as I followed him out of the room.

Ten

With the low sun in their tired red eyes, Dan and Gavin walked down the main street of Byron Bay towards the beach, Dan fiddling nervously with the bundle of plastic bank notes in his pocket. There was a brief moment of consideration to stop for food at the bakery, but what they both really wanted was a proper English kebab.

The pair had been clubbing all night and had yet to go back to their campsite, deciding instead to score more coke and try to keep going throughout the next twenty-four hours, through the evening parade and live gigs dotted around the town, right up until sun rise on New Year's Day.

Watching as a couple of dreadlocked surfers jogged past them, boards under their arms, Dan muttered *'losers'* under his breath, just loud enough for Gavin to hear him, drawing a snigger from his cousin. If there was anything they hated about backpacking, it was the tree hugging, longhaired hippies and surfers that seemed to plague them everywhere they went. As if it wasn't bad enough that Thailand was full of cretins trying to *find themselves*, they'd found that Australia also had plenty of those plus hundreds of *surf dudes*, pretentiously swanning around, acting like the sun shone out of their arses just because they played in the waves.

Despite the scum they were surrounded by, Dan and Gavin had been enjoying a great time away in Thailand, especially around the full moon party. Every night they'd each enjoyed the company of a different prostitute, young and old, one of which sorted them out with some drugs for the full moon party. Those drugs then funded further nights of sordid pleasure when they sold off most of them to fellow backpackers. If only Australia was as good and simple. Everything here was expensive, too expensive. Scoring decent drugs wasn't too difficult at least, but it certainly wasn't as cheap as they'd been led to believe it would be.

Grinding his teeth, Dan glanced around for the rusty old van with yellow flowers painted all over it. It was a feral hippy truck, there was no doubt about that, but they did have some great products on sale and right now, Dan and Gavin couldn't care less who they were buying from as long as they got what they needed. The van however, had moved on since the previous evening, the space now empty, leaving them cursing as they continued walking hoping it hadn't gone too far.

Waking up alone in her small house, Isabella wondered again if it was time to leave Byron Bay. The months she'd spent there had been great but she'd hardly seen anything else in Australia and there was so much more she wanted to take in before her trip was over.

The last time she'd mentioned that to Ambur, the Byron Bay local had been keen to join her on a road trip across the vast country, but that was when Josh was in Fiji and Ambur wasn't sure if he'd be back in town. Now that Josh was not only back in town but had picked up where he had left off with Ambur, Isabella worried that their road trip was going to be sacrificed.

The other thing that had been on her mind was Matt. She'd fallen for him at first sight during her house party and had been impressed that he seemed to be going slow with her rather than pouncing the first chance he had. But then Ambur's colleague had told her about Matt's little challenge set by his friends back home and how Matt, and his two Canadian friends, had been joking about him needing a third notch on his belt by New Year's Day. Sickened by the thought that Matt was only after one thing, Isabella knew she'd been right to snub him.

That had been before Noodle was forced to swim out and rescue Matt from the stormy surf, at which point Isabella had realised that she still cared about him. It was also before Josh, who had only known Matt a couple of days, stood up for him, agreeing that the bet was the sort of thing he and his friends would have done. Even Ambur, her best friend who'd told her of the situation in the first place, had suggested she give Matt a second chance and the opportunity to prove that he wasn't in it for the bet.

With all these things running through her mind, she couldn't get back to sleep, and decided instead to get up and join Lola and Ambur for a morning yoga session on the beach.

Lighting up yet another cigarette to help her deal with the problems that had so unfairly been dealt to her, Claire inhaled a long drag and focused on the distant surfers that seemed to be madly battling against a constant stream of incoming waves. Despite being in Byron Bay with her boyfriend Brent, she felt both bored and trapped by the small town. Although Byron Bay wasn't really the problem, it

137

was Brent. Back in England he'd been amazing, Mr Perfect, despite his occasional jealous fits. Claire figured he only acted that way because he loved her; if he didn't care about her then he would have been blasé about who looked at her, or who she spoke to. Since he'd flown to Thailand to surprise her, he'd hardly let her out of his sight and yet was becoming increasingly difficult to want around. All Claire wanted to do was relax and read, all Brent wanted to do was find a bar with sports on the TV and get drunk. That would have been fine, except Claire had to accompany him wherever he went, meaning she couldn't just chill out and relax. Added to which, he didn't even seem interested in having sex with her anymore. There had been times in the past week, like now, when she'd managed to escape him for a few minutes, telling him she was popping out for cigarettes and instead heading down to the beach for a moment alone. Although already in the past few minutes, he'd sent three text messages to her phone.

As she sat contemplating the past few weeks, Claire realised that she needed to get rid of Brent. Her feelings for Matt, she knew, had moved beyond simple lust. In Thailand he'd been an adventurous and promiscuous relationship, in which she knew she could call the shots and dominate their decisions and that was in a sense what she now craved. She knew that given the right circumstances she could easily seduce him again, their kiss outside the bakery days earlier had proven that, however her time to act on her feelings was running out and she knew Brent would be watching.

The waves were bigger than Rhoda was hoping for, but after having waited the past two days for the ocean to calm down she welcomed the chance to swim in the warm sea, not having been in the water since her night snorkel on Koh Phi Phi. As she felt the water push and pull her around as the waves came crashing in, Rhoda had a brief moment of panic when she realised she couldn't touch the sandy bottom, moments before a large wave crashed onto her, pushing her down beneath the surface. As she desperately swam for the shore, taking in gulps of saltwater, her feet finally graced the bottom and with a struggle she managed to edge her way in, throwing harsh looks at the nearby lifeguard for his worthless presence.

Glancing over she could see that her two roommates had been blissfully unaware of her fright as they lay playing cards, a nearby palm shading them from the bright midday sun. Exhausted, she walked back over to them, sitting back down on her sarong and letting out an almighty sigh as she attempted to gain some sympathy from her new friends. The effort was lost, as neither one of them took the slightest notice, immersed in their cards as always. It wasn't so unexpected. In the few days since she'd arrived from Brisbane, she'd had to force herself upon Ryan and Scott in an effort to be social, even playing cards with them for hours on end during the previous two nights. However, it was becoming quite apparent that unless she was willing to join in and play cards, they weren't too interested in her company.

'I almost drowned,' Rhoda said, as she watched the Canadians study their cards.

'Really?' Scott said.

'Yeah, not that either of you seem bothered,' she said.

'Well, that's what the lifeguard is there for. Did he save you?' Ryan replied as he glanced up for a brief moment.

'Yeah, he swam in and saved me, giving me mouth to mouth,' she replied, watching them continue, clearly not listening to her. 'Do you guys fancy doing something other than playing cards?' she asked.

'Like what?' Scott asked.

'Like... Oh, I don't know, we could go shopping, go for a coffee, go for a walk up to the lighthouse,' Rhoda replied.

'Not really, I'm cool just chilling out,' Ryan replied, as Scott nodded along with him.

'Well you are exciting, coming all this way to Australia just to play cards. I don't suppose you've heard from your mate yet?' Rhoda asked. The past couple of days, the Canadians had been telling her they'd be spending New Year's Eve with an English friend but so far he'd been oddly elusive, causing Rhoda to question his existence.

'What Matt?' Scott asked, making Rhoda once again think of her brief fling with the same name in Thailand, although she knew that it couldn't possibly be the same guy she'd met, as by now he would be back in England. 'He'll be around some point later I reckon,' he casually replied.

Walking down the beach to check the surf Noodle was lost in his thoughts, thankful for the time alone. The past year had been a walking nightmare for him, having attempted suicide surfing on the impossibly shallow Indonesian reefs. There had then followed whole weeks lost in the bottom of a whisky bottle, only to pick himself up for a couple of months before losing the plot once again.

The only positive aspect of the whole year had been meeting Lola. She had come into his life at a time when he'd hit another low, barely venturing out of his Danang guesthouse, his mind torn by guilt and self-loathing. But instead of ignoring him, she'd reached out, offering a friendly ear and non-judgmental conversation for the first time in months.

The more time he'd spent with Lola, the more he learnt about her own background and the guilt she carried surrounding her father's death when she was younger. And it was that common bond that snapped Noodle out of his dark mood, agreeing to join her as she headed back to Thailand.

By the time they'd reached Koh Phi Phi, Noodle was starting to sink again though, pulled back by Matt, an unlikely kid, who as well as being Lola's old friend, seemed to be as keen to try his luck against the natural elements as Noodle himself. Although it was clear that Matt didn't quite yet have the know-how to make the best use of his pluck, Noodle could see a certain amount of his old self in the kid, which made him unusually warm to him.

Knowing the year was nearly out, all Noodle wanted was to finish it with a perfect surf, the absence of which he'd recently realised had contributed to his downfall. In his mind he knew that travelling to New Zealand with Lola was the right thing to do. There would be good waves there and he'd have the space to try and get back into writing, maybe even find himself somewhere near where he'd been before Fran's death.

As Noodle reached the main beach, he couldn't believe his luck. The breezy wind was offshore, holding ten-foot faces left over from the recent swell creating some stunning barrelling waves. It was better than he could possibly have hoped for.

Wasting no time watching the surf, Noodle turned around and ran barefoot back towards Liquid Dreams, feeling energised not only by the thought of the waves, but happy for once, that he'd have some friends to surf them with.

Continuing their search along the seafront for the flowery yellow van or its bohemian residents, Dan and Gavin were getting more than a little edgy. It had been hours since their last line of coke and they desperately needed something to help take the edge off. Otherwise it was only a matter of time until they'd need to head back to their tent and crash out, especially with the midday sun bearing down on them.

Deciding to abandon the road altogether and wander down onto the beach, hoping to catch a whiff of a joint and source another dealer, the guys were dumbstruck to find a familiar face walking out of the ocean, just a few metres ahead of them. Stood frozen on the spot, the pair racked their brains trying to remember her name, but all they could recall was the young guy she was with and how they'd purposely broken into her room and stolen his bag, out of spite after the blonde rejected Dan at the full moon party.

'Hi,' Dan said, smiling, as he stepped directly in Claire's path.
'*Hi?*' she replied, trying hard to place the man's sunburnt face but thinking the tattoo of the bulldog on his friend looked familiar.
'Dan and Gavin... From Koh Pha Ngan, remember?' Dan prompted. As she heard their names, a slight chill ran up her naked spine, the face she could now picture as belonging to the man who'd sold her the diet pills and had been stalking her throughout the full moon party as she'd danced with Matt. Taking a nervous step back towards the ocean and glancing over Dan's shoulder hoping to catch Brent's eye, she recalled the hazy memories of the night in her head. Shortly after Matt had disappeared, Dan had approached, trying to kiss her, but Claire still had enough control of the situation to get away. That was just before Brent had texted to say he was in Thailand.
'I remember,' she coldly replied, putting her arms across her chest. 'What do you want?'
'Just being friendly, slim chances running into you again, huh?' Dan replied. 'So where's your boyfriend gone to?' Gavin asked.
'I'm right here, can I help?' Brent angrily asked, stood behind the two lads and expanding his rugby playing frame, as he squared up to Dan.
'Who the *fuck* are you?' Gavin asked the stranger that was threatening his friend, as he clenched his right fist in anticipation.
'Her *boyfriend*, who the fuck are *you?*' Brent spat.
'We're old friends of your lovely lady here, although you're *not* the boyfriend I met,' Dan said, winking at Claire before backing off and walking away back up the beach.

Watching the two strangers head off down the beach and his girlfriend slink off towards their spot on the beach, Brent remained planted to the spot, feeling the adrenaline of his anger pumping through his veins, Dan's words *not the boyfriend I met* rushing through his mind. Walking back up towards Claire, his hands remained clenched as though he still planned on punching something, only relaxing them as he sat down, his body still tense with rage.

'So, you want to tell me who your *friends* were?' Brent snapped at Claire after seconds of silence.

'I don't know, just a couple of leering arseholes, I guess,' Claire replied, lighting up a cigarette.

'So you don't know them?' Brent asked in disbelief.

'*No!*' Claire protested.

'Well they seemed to know you. Who do you suppose he meant was your *other boyfriend* then?'

'Look, I don't know them, so I don't know what the *fuck* they meant by that. At a guess I'd say they were just winding you up and by the look on your face, I'd say it worked. Why don't you try and trust me, just for once, instead of jumping to conclusions and being such a prick all the time,' Claire argued, as she began fumbling about for her things, collecting them up to head back to the hostel and away from Brent.

'Where are you going?' he asked.

'Back to the hostel and away from you,' she said.

'Back to your *other boyfriend*, perhaps? I don't think so Claire - I'm not an idiot. Why don't you just stay and relax, otherwise we're both going back to the hostel, which would be a shame on such a sunny day,' Brent said, his tone becoming more friendly as he gently held Claire's wrist to stop her packing.

Sat on his surfboard, during what Noodle knew would be his last surf of the year if not his last ever in Byron Bay, he couldn't help wish that Steve was out in the water with him. The weathered old surfer had reluctantly declined to join them, having instead to man the fort at Liquid Dreams. As one of his old friends who had helped him get through the first few months following Fran's death, Noodle was at least certain that they'd surf together some place other than Byron Bay and with a contented smile he took off on another wave and promptly pulled into the small barrel it created for him.

'Noodle! Last wave dude,' Josh called out to his friend as he watched an incoming set, paddling for position to catch the first wave. Instinctively, Josh took a few powerful strokes, before he sprang to his feet and gracefully carved a big turn across the face of the blue wall of water that was rising up before him. Suddenly changing speed, his board whipped up at the top of the wave, causing a perfect arc of water to spray up, before he turned his board towards the beach and let the crumbling line of white water carry him in.

Messing about in the small waves near the shoreline, Matt watched his friends' manoeuvres in the bigger surf with great interest. With every session he felt himself improving and anticipated the day he too would be catching and riding waves with such ease. For the time being though, he was resigned to the fact that surfing, just like women, would remain an intricate undertaking that only time might earn him any real level of understanding and success with.

Only a couple of days ago Matt had felt that everything was perfectly mapped out for a great New Year's Eve party. However, since Isabella had learnt of his childish bet it had all become blurred and potholed. Romantically, his chances with her had been damaged beyond repair and although he thought he could quite easily gain a celebratory snog from a drunken stranger during the night, he didn't really want to kiss just a stranger. He was still infatuated by Isabella and her aversion to him only seemed to strengthen that, which was why he'd decided to make a special effort to track down the Canadians, Ryan and Scott, despite not having seen them for a few days. As far as he could see, without their company things would get awkward with Isabella as the others coupled off.

Looking out through the grubby communal kitchen window, Ryan noticed that the early evening sky was beginning to cloud over with threatening dark clouds. Over the past few weeks of thinking about spending New Year's Eve in Byron Bay, amid the outdoor festivities, the weather wasn't something either he or Scott had given any thought to, both assuming that it would be warm and dry. Potential rain clouds certainly weren't mentioned in the plan that Matt had relayed to him a couple of hours earlier either when, making a brief escape from Rhoda, the two Canadians had gone to Liquid Dreams in the hope of finding their buddy. Discussing their plans, they'd consciously overlooked Rhoda's addition to their number when talking to Matt, in the hope that she might find someone else to cling to for the night, and as the evening began to draw in, it seemed like their Irish roommate might well have done just that, having been missing the past few hours.

Although beer was always their drink of choice, Scott had earlier pointed out the signs around town, warning that the streets were to be alcohol-free for the night. So they'd come up with the plan to add rum into plastic coke bottles, giving the impression to onlookers that they were only drinking cola. As they went about mixing their concoctions on the veranda, the rain began to fall, first lightly and then it hammered down on the roof, mixed with flashes of lightning and deep rumbling thunder that drowned out the communal radio nearby.

As they continued to monitor the weather and mix their drinks, they discussed Rhoda again and decided that they couldn't leave her without a single friend on New Year's Eve. So figuring that the rain might have stopped before she returned, they drew a copy of the map Matt had provided for them, showing the way to Isabella's house, along with their phone numbers, and left the instructions on her bed.

Glancing over the edge of the veranda railing, they could see that the road was already submerged in a large shallow puddle and suddenly the outdoor festivities really didn't seem like such a good idea. Sitting down, Scott produced a deck of cards from his pocket and proceeded to shuffle, with the shared unspoken intention of waiting at the hostel until the rain stopped.

Sat alone on the beach, pondering the year ahead, Rhoda watched the dark clouds moving ever closer across the ocean. Taking a long drag on her crudely rolled joint, she thought she saw a flash of lightning out of the corner of her eye to the left. She fixed her gaze in that direction for a moment before another bright flash lit up the whole sky and rain starting to come down all around her.

Flicking the joint away onto the dark, damp sand, Rhoda quickly got to her feet, heading towards the nearby car park where a large stage had earlier been erected, looking for shelter and increasing her pace as the rain came down harder. There were at least a hundred people gathered around the stage area but they all dispersed and ran for shelter as Rhoda drew closer, her clothes already soaked through to her skin.

The rain held her prisoner outside a small shop, as she sheltered beneath the awning and wrung out her blue top. The salad sandwich she'd taken down to the beach for dinner had filled the gap in her stomach, but now an attack of the munchies was steadily creeping up on her. Looking around, every shop was closed, even the bakery that she'd discovered the day before was having its annual day off. So it seemed her best bet would be to scrounge a little something off her two Canadian friends, the names of whom she kept on getting mixed up. Spending New Year with them both, together with their friends, wasn't an ideal scenario but certainly more preferable than spending it alone and besides the book she'd just been reading promoted the idea of destiny, so she figured something great may come of it all.

When finally the downpour eased off enough for her to make a dash through the puddles and back to her hostel, she swiftly took off her flip-flops and ran down the street on her tender bare feet, the rain finally stopping as she turned the corner to the hostel.

Heading straight for her room to dry off, Rhoda decided to avoid embarrassment, given her drenched state, and avoided the communal areas. Entering the dorm room, there was no sign of either Canadian but thankfully they'd left a small map on her bed revealing their whereabouts. Peeling off her dripping clothes and towelling herself down, she picked up the dry red and white patterned sarong she'd used as a ground sheet on the beach earlier in the day and wrapped it around her slender waist creating a skirt. Pulling a creased black vest top out of her backpack and over her head, slipping back into her wet flip-flops, reapplying her make-up in front of the tiny room mirror, Rhoda then patted her wet scraggly hair down and slid a red hairclip in. Her transformation was complete, all in less than five minutes.

Digging about in her bag for the evening's ecstasy pill and placing it down her bra for safekeeping, she picked up the map and headed out of the dorm, bypassing the communal areas again, and ventured out into the warm night in search of the party.

Claire had silently watched with bitterness, as Matt and his two friends left the hostel. Judging by their smiles and laughter, they were in for a good night and yet hadn't even bothered to invite her and Brent along or wish them a Happy New Year. This was something that also infuriated Brent somewhat as he couldn't see any reason for their snub - they'd all spent Christmas Day together and gotten along well so why not invite them along for New Year? Claire, on the other hand, enviously knew their cold shoulder had to be something to do with the Spanish girl she'd seen Matt getting close to at Christmas.

Pouring another strong serving of vodka into her glass, Claire glared across the table at her brutish boyfriend and tried to work out what had attracted her to him in the first place. How he'd ever trusted her enough to fly off around the other side of the planet and leave her alone at home was a complete mystery, although in his absence she knew his friends had been keeping an eye on her.

Now that the rain had stopped, all Claire wanted to do was leave the hostel and get lost among the masses of people filling up the streets of Byron Bay, but she knew it was too early to work her plan, especially as Matt had just headed out. So she patiently waited, smoking cigarette after cigarette, while Brent tried his best to drink as many beers as possible in the small space of time before they left.

Inside Isabella's house for the first time in days, Matt felt a little awkward being back, however if Isabella still had any ill feeling towards him, she wasn't showing it, but then as Josh had pointed out she wasn't giving him *vibes* anymore either. Hearing a knock on the door and expecting it to be the Canadians, Matt pulled himself up off the comfortable cushions and walked over to answer it. As he pulled the door open, stood before him was a familiar face that he'd never expected, or hoped, to see again.

As Matt and Rhoda stood gawping at each other, Matt briefly wondered if he was hallucinating from the joint he'd just been smoking, thinking for a moment of shutting the door and reopening it to see if his Irish one night stand was still at Isabella's door. There was absolutely no reason that she would or could be, not only was she was meant to be in Brisbane, but surely somebody would have mentioned inviting a friend called Rhoda, such an unusual name that would have rung alarm bells in his head.

There was nothing else to do. Matt closed the door, just as Rhoda was about to speak. He then took a deep breath and reopened it, shocked to find she was still standing there, confused.

'Rhoda?' Matt tentatively asked, now considering the idea of poking her to see if she was real.

'Matt?' she replied, seemingly just as lost for words '...I'm err... looking for two friends of mine Scott and Ryan, they drew me this map, I must have come to the wrong place,' she said, thrusting the map forwards for Matt's examination, but it was a replica of the one that he'd drawn for them, he recognised that instantly. As he stood silently contemplating why the Canadians would have given Rhoda instructions to find him, Josh came over to the door to see who the visitor was.

'Hi,' Josh said.

'Hi, I er…' Rhoda started, looking at Matt who seemed lost in thought, before continuing, 'I'm looking for my friends Scott and Ryan, they drew me this map,' she said, thrusting the map to Josh, who quickly inspected it.

'Yeah, you mean the Canadian guys?' Josh replied.

'Yes!' she exclaimed. 'One's smart the other scruffy,' Rhoda said.

'Well you've come to the right place, they should be here pretty soon, huh Matt?' Josh asked, breaking Matt's thoughts.

'Er… Yeah, should be,' Matt replied.

'Cool, well come in. I'm Josh, this is Matt. *I think he's maybe had a little too much to smoke.*' Josh whispered to Rhoda. 'Come on, move Matt, let the lady in,' he said, gently pushing Matt to the side to let Rhoda pass.

Sitting down on the cushions beside Isabella, Rhoda couldn't help but feel she'd been transported into a twilight zone. In the small room was not only Matt, who was meant to be back in England, but another woman who she was sure she recognised from a dive shop in Koh Phi Phi. Yet, the Canadians that she was meant to be meeting were nowhere to be seen.

As introductions went around the room, Rhoda couldn't help but reflect on her book, which would have said that her being there was destiny rather than sheer coincidence. However, stealing a glance back towards her potential soul mate, she couldn't help but think that if Matt was really *the one*, then surely she would have found him more attractive. He wasn't really her type and definitely younger looking than she'd soberly have gone for.

Sat uncomfortably across from Rhoda, Matt tried to remain calm, ignoring her as much as he could in the hope that she wouldn't ask him why he was back in Australia, or mention any of the things he'd laid claim to the night they had met. However, as bad as the situation was, he knew that it would be much worse when the Canadians arrived and discovered that he and Rhoda knew each other. Perhaps not only innocently point out that he was a fresh-faced backpacker but also realise that Rhoda was in fact one of his two conquests, which had the potential for really big trouble. So, when Noodle suggested they get going and head into town, Matt couldn't have been happier; he could now try and lose Rhoda, or at least answer her questions with more lies in private.

Stepping out of the house, Rhoda noticed with a smile, that the puddles had begun to disperse and the sky had cleared. The whereabouts of Ryan and Scott was a concern, she had their phone numbers but no phone and nobody else, not even Matt, seemed too bothered about their absence.

Under the weight of his small rucksack, Josh began to wonder just what he'd been thinking of when he'd agreed to carry a dozen bottles of beer on his back for the group. Not only was a random bottle digging into his spine with every step but the possibility of dancing was out of the question, at least until more of the beer was drunk or they'd been caught and had them taken away.

'So Rhoda,' Matt said, once he knew he was out of earshot from the others. 'I thought you were spending New Year in Brisbane.'
'I was, but decided I would head to the beach for a few days. Fingers crossed after this, I'm going to go back and look for a job,' she smiled. 'What are you doing here though, I thought you'd be back in England by now. I must say it was quite a shock to see you open the door.'
'It was a little odd yeah,' Matt smiled, hoping he hadn't looked too alarmed. 'It's a bit of a strange story really,' he said, still trying to formulate it in his head. 'I was about to fly back when I'd heard my Aunt who lives over here had taken a turn for the worse. As I was relatively close by, my parents offered to pay for me to fly back to Sydney to help out.'
'That's terrible,' she solemnly nodded.
'Yeah, but then by the time I'd reached Sydney she was almost fine, having made a miracle recovery, apparently.'
'Oh wow!' Rhoda said.
'So, she seemed to be okay and insisted I spend New Year here, but I'm going to head back down to Sydney and check up on her in a couple of days, just to make sure she's alright.'
'That's so sweet of you,' she replied, impressed by his compassion.
'I was also thinking of sticking around in Australia for a bit longer as I've got a new visa, but I don't think I'll be going back up Brisbane way again, unfortunately,' he added.
'Really? That's too bad, well if you change your mind, it would always be nice to see you,' she replied, thinking that he couldn't possibly be the one, if they were again destined to go in different directions.

Drunkenly slapping a king of clubs down on the large wooden table, Ryan smiled with glee at winning his sixth straight game of

148

shithead. The mixed contents of his cola bottle were almost gone in the seemingly short time they'd been playing cards. Likewise, Scott's drink was down to the final few mouthfuls, but unlike his friend, he'd begun to realise that the pair were now alone in what was a busy veranda. As Ryan began to shuffle the cards out for another round, Scott got up and looked over the veranda railing. The rain had stopped, the sky was now clear and the pool of rainwater that once covered the entire paving area outside had now dried up.

'What's the time buddy?' Scott asked, still leaning over the balcony, now able to hear the beat of music playing in the distance.

'Eleven fif... *oh shit*! It's eleven-fifteen! ... We were supposed to be meeting Matt at eight!' Ryan exclaimed from across the deserted room. 'What are we going to do?'

'What do you think? Grab your liquor and lets roll into town before we miss the whole party,' Scott announced, picking up his own drink and promptly heading for the exit.

The road leading from the Canadians' hostel was abandoned, but turning onto Jonson Street, seconds later the pair were surrounded by thousands. All around them were uninhibited revellers, dancers, jugglers, fire-breathers and drummers blended in with children, grandparents and the inebriated. The dress code was anything and everything, from body paint, to fancy dress, casual surf to glam. The party had already kicked off without them hours earlier with a big parade, and now they were thrust right into the mix, beside a stage with a reggae band playing.

They passed by the masses towards the main stage, which was in the car park beside the beach where they'd remembered Matt was planning to spend the countdown. Ryan followed his friend closely through the labyrinth of people, but as he felt a strong hand lay upon his shoulder from behind, he stopped his friend and turned around to face the hand's owner.

'This is an alcohol-free zone mate,' a uniformed policeman bluntly explained as he looked down at Ryan's nearly empty coke bottle.

'Okay thanks,' Ryan replied before trying to turn away, but again he felt the hand back on his shoulder.

'You're going to have to hand over your booze lads,' the policeman shouted into Ryan's ear, just to make sure he understood.

'What booze? What this?' Ryan asked defensively, as he held up his soft drink bottle.

'That's right and yours mate,' the policeman said, nodding towards Scott's bottle.

'It's only soda pop, not alcohol,' Ryan lied as he begrudgingly handed over his drink.

'Really?' The policeman asked as he unscrewed the cap and took a sniff. 'Smells like whisky.'

'Whisky? Oh come on buddy, *it's not whisky*, that stuff tastes like shit, give me *some* credit,' Ryan argued, but it was too late and he watched with a pained expression as the remains of his drink were tipped out into a nearby drain, before the policeman repeated the process with Scott's.

Trudging on, reeling from having lost their drink, the Canadians reached the main stage, or as close as they could get. There were thousands of moving bodies all jostling and dancing for a place around the car park. At its heart a DJ was spinning her tunes, the bass line reverberating as it boomed out through the masses. Beyond was a dramatic backdrop of crashing waves and illuminating forks of lightning from a distant storm that ravaged out over the Pacific Ocean.

Looking around the heaving crowd, Claire realised that her time for escape from Brent had come, but as the alcohol took a firmer grasp on her senses, she decided not only to lose him for the night, but for good. Lighting up a cigarette in anticipation of the stress that was sure to follow, Claire led her boyfriend away from the crowds and loud speakers to a spot of grass where she hoped she'd be heard and more importantly understood.

'Are you alright?' he asked before letting out a noisy beer-induced belch.

'No Brent!' she started, 'I'm not, I haven't been since Thailand or maybe you haven't noticed,' she said, forcefully blowing out a lungful of smoke.

'I've noticed you haven't been too happy but that's just homesickness, you'll be alright in a few weeks.'

'*Homesickness*? Brent are you *blind*? The problem is *you*, pure and simple. You're an overprotective prick who gets mad whenever I talk to any other man,' Claire said.

'Oh, what, like those guys down at the beach this afternoon? They were just perverts,' Brent said, feeling a mixture of anger and astonishment at Claire's words.

'*Yes*, like today but you know what? *I did know them*. The tall one you threatened, tried to kiss me the night you arrived in Koh Pha Ngan,' Claire said, feeling an enormous weight lift off her shoulders.

'*What*! Oh man, I'm going to *fuck* that guy up!' Brent said, playing straight into her hands.

'...And he was right, *I did* have another boyfriend...and Matt was a much better shag than you too,' Claire said, wanting to hurt Brent with her words, but as soon they had left her lips she wanted to grab each and every one and force them back inside her mouth, but it was too late.

'You did *what*? Who's this Matt?' he demanded.

'Who do you think?' Claire cried.

'Surely *not* the Matt from Liquid Dreams?' Brent shouted. Pulling at his short hair in desperation, but Claire's look of panic and the tears that ran down her cheeks, told him all that he needed to know. 'Oh, you are something else, *you bitch*! Fuck the guy from the beach, I'm going to pound the crap out of that little shit Matt...You and me are *over* Claire and believe me if you ever see your precious little *Matt* again, you won't recognise his broken face,' Brent spat, before storming off into the crowd.

Falling to her knees, Claire stubbed her cigarette out on the wet grass, before digging around in her bag for another one and lighting up with shaking hands. She'd been expecting to feel elated at the prospect of finding herself single again, but as dark mascara-filled tears ran down her face, she felt empty. She didn't regret breaking up, but as she glanced towards the crowds she suddenly felt all alone, needing desperately to find the one that could make her smile again, the same person that her deranged ex-boyfriend had a head start in finding.

The drum and bass music that the current DJ played behind him wasn't really to Matt's tastes, but he found it surprisingly easy to lose himself in the quick beat. Despite the disappointing no-show of Ryan and Scott, and the surprising appearance of Rhoda, he felt the night was going better than he'd thought possible, especially as Isabella was actually dancing with him and flashing the occasional sexy smile his way.

As Matt moved away from the dance area, heading towards the nearby toilets, a group of fire twirlers began to show off their talents right in his path, so he edged his way around, pushing through the crowd that had turned to watch the pyromaniacs doing their sideshow.

Matt could smell the toilet before he had even reached the door, but reaching out to pull it open, he spotted something familiar out of the corner of his eye, his heart suddenly thudding heavily in his chest. Strapped to the back of a stranger was his bag, not the big one that he had left in his dorm room but the smaller one that had been taken from his room in Thailand. Turning away from the toilet door, Matt cut through the crowd following the bag, which as he got closer, was undoubtedly his. Written across the top was the word *mellow*, some of the Tipp-Ex had been worn away but it was still prominent enough to show his writing. Without hesitating, Matt moved quickly through the crowd in the hope that he might determine the identity of the thief. Before he got a chance to get close, the thief turned around and revealed himself. Matt recognised the man and his companion but couldn't think where he knew them from. Stood frozen in the moving crowd, eyes fixated on the pair, Matt clicked, they'd been in Koh Pha Ngan, they'd sold Claire her drugs and he realised they must, that night, have stolen his bag, knowing he and Claire were out at the party. As he took it all in, Matt decided to back off a little, hoping that he wasn't recognised by them as he tried to figure out the best way to retrieve his bag.

There was no way that Matt could overpower both of them and get his bag back, he knew he needed his friends and seeing the fire twirlers to his left, Matt knew that they couldn't be far away. However, he realised that if he went to find the others and lost sight of the bag, he might never see it again. So circling the pair for a minute, feeling the adrenaline pump through his veins, he tried to figure out a way to find his friends without losing sight of his bag.

The rage was unbearable inside Brent's head. At no point, as he pushed and shoved his way through the crowd, could he make any sense of how scrawny Matt could have possibly pulled his Claire. However, he needed to lash out at someone, and if Matt was really the backstabbing bastard that Claire had claimed he was, then he would have to pay for it with flesh.

In the sea of thousands Brent knew that the search might continue until the morning, but he was prepared to keep going until justice was served. There was only so long Matt could remain elusive, as after all, Brent knew where he was staying. However, as he wandered around the sea of strangers, being pushed and shoved around by mindless, intoxicated revellers the frustration was becoming irrepressible and it was going to need to be released sooner rather than later, whether he found Matt or just got pushed one too many times.

Moving past a group of fire twirlers, a wicked snarl replaced the frown on Brent's face, as not more than ten-feet ahead, stood his target. Matt, he could see, was gazing his way but fixed on a point between them, seemingly lost in his thoughts. Without hesitation, Brent rushed forwards and with unexpected force shoved a guy in his way, down to the floor. Moments later, just a few feet from Matt, Brent was stopped in his tracks by a strong hand grabbing his collar.

It all happened in a blur, watching the two guys with his bag, Matt saw the shorter of the two suddenly being pushed to the ground. As he watched the other one, bag still on his shoulders, grab the guy who'd pushed his friend, Matt realised with horror that it was Brent.

Matt watched on, as just feet away Brent turned and threw a head punch at the bag thief, knocking him back a couple of feet, before he turned back to face Matt, fiery eyes full of rage as he made a step towards him, only to be knocked sideways by the guy he'd first thrown to the floor.

As the crowd around them took a step back, Matt watched as the two guys took on the larger Brent, all three men were throwing around punches. Their faces bloodied in seconds as they shuffled around, each trying to gain the best ground upon his opponent. Beyond them on the floor, Matt realised that the thief had discarded his bag which lay on the other side of the ruckus.

As Matt began to edge around the fighters to reach his bag, he watched as Brent knocked the smaller of his opponents out cold onto the hard bitumen, before looking up and again, spotting Matt in the crowd and making a lunge towards him, only to be stopped again by the bag thief, grabbing Brent with an arm around his neck, pulling him backwards away from the startled onlookers.

As Matt watched on, frozen to the spot just feet away from his bag, he glanced up through the scattered crowd and saw a number of uniformed police swiftly making their way towards them. Realising that it was his only chance, Matt stepped towards the fighters who were now both on the ground, throwing tired punches at one another and hastily grabbed the strap of his bag, dragging it along the ground to his feet.

A second later, a dozen policemen were all around them, some seizing the fighters and tearing them apart whilst the others dispersed the stunned crowd. As he backed away Matt took a final glance down at the handcuffed men, picked up his bag and turned to vanish into the crowd, puzzled by what he'd just witnessed.

Moving back to the less crowded toilet area, Matt was suddenly confronted by Claire. Looking dishevelled, her knees and skirt were muddy, her make-up had run and she seemed panicky as she took his hand and led him away.

'Are you alright Claire?' Matt asked as he followed her.

'Brent's looking for you Matt,' she said.

'*Brent*?'

'Yeah, he's really angry, I think he wants to hurt you?'

'What?' Matt said, wondering if she knew about the fight.

'I'm really sorry but I told him about us. Then he just stormed off,' she said, lighting up a cigarette.

'I just saw him,' Matt said. 'He was in a fight.'

'*What*? A fight with *who*?' Claire asked, looking over Matt's shoulder for a sign of Brent.

'Strangely enough, with the guys from Thailand that sold you those drugs and stole my bag,' Matt said, pulling his *mellow* bag round to show her. 'Look, I got it back,' he beamed.

'He didn't hit you?' she asked, ignoring the bag.

'No, I think he may have tried though. I think he took a pretty good beating, last I saw he was being taken away in handcuffs.'

'He's been arrested?' Claire asked, feeling a mixture of horror and relief that the man she'd loved was in police custody.

'I think so… But why the *hell* did you tell him about us, surely you knew he'd come after me?' Matt quizzed.

'I'm sorry,' Claire said, her tears welling up. 'I wasn't thinking, I wanted to dump him and I figured that would send the message home.'

'What? By getting me pounded into oblivion? Thanks!' Matt said, thinking he'd heard enough and just wanted to get away from her.

'I did it for *us*,' she cried as Matt turned away.

'Did *what* for us?'

'I'm single now, I want to pick up where we left off on the island,' she said.

'What?' Matt said, as he turned to face her again, only to be pulled forwards by her hands around his shoulders, bringing him in for a passionate kiss.

As Matt gave into the kiss, he had the feeling that he was being watched and broke it off; glancing round to find Isabella stood watching him. 'Isabella!' Matt called out as he pushed Claire away, shouldered the bag and darted off, leaving Claire desperately calling out to him.

Matt kept sight of Isabella as she weaved her way through the crowd but as he came to the end of the car park, where the beach started and the streetlights failed to illuminate, she had vanished from view. He knew she'd gone down onto the sand, but he was faced with a choice of left or right. As he stood contemplating a sudden flash of lightning showed the outline of her slight figure. Running, as fast as he could with the heavy bag, Matt soon caught up to her who, upon realising she'd been found, sat down on the damp sand.

'What is it you want from me Matt?' she asked quietly, remaining focused upon the ocean.

'I want to explain. I didn't kiss her, *she kissed me*,' Matt pleaded.

'Are you really that desperate to screw a third before the morning comes?' she asked, unaware of his history with Claire.

'What? *No*, I tried to tell you days ago, that I'm not even thinking about that. I really don't care about it.'

'But I've seen how she looks at you, you could have had her?' she said.

'I don't *want* her,' Matt replied.

'So, what do you want?' she repeated.

'Right now, I want you to accept my apology for all that has happened between us. I want the opportunity to start afresh, just as friends,' he replied, watching another bolt of lightning flash beyond the crashing waves.

'*Just friends*? You don't want anything more than that between us?' she asked.

'*No*... well *yes*, but I know it'll never happen, so no. I'd rather settle to be your friend than lose you completely,' he replied, as silence fell between them.

'Apology accepted,' Isabella finally said, turning and smiling at Matt, who was still fixated on the ocean.

'What?' he asked, unsure that he'd heard her right.

'I said, I accept your apology,' she repeated. 'On three conditions.'

'Okay...' Matt said, turning to face her. 'Go on.'

'Number one, you call me Issi. That's what my friends call me.'

'No problem, *Issi*,' Matt smiled.

'Number two, if you ever lie to me or hurt me again, I swear I'll kick you so hard in the nuts, you'll spend the rest of your life with an ice pack down your shorts,' she said.

'*Right*,' he replied, wincing at the thought.

'Number three... I get a kiss,' she said, taking him by surprise as she slowly leaned in to kiss him.

With just two minutes left in the year, Lola anxiously looked down at her watch again. She hadn't seen Matt for nearly an hour since he'd walked off to find a toilet and then there had been the brief drama where, from what she could make out, a squad of policemen had broken up a fight. Matt wasn't the fighting sort, she knew that, but all the same she worried about whether or not he'd somehow become caught up in the brawl.

Expressing her concern to Ambur and Josh, the three of them noticed that Isabella had also been missing a while and, reluctant to move until the New Year had been called in, they agreed to launch a search party as soon as the celebrations were all over. Sure enough, as the final ten seconds of the year began to ring out around the town, Matt emerged hand in hand with Isabella. Following closely behind them were the Canadian guys having eventually found Matt.

As the last second ticked away, masses of people erupted in a simultaneous and energetic blast of cheers. Fists were raised towards the night sky and every pair of eyes moved to another's, looking to share their joy of a new year with a celebratory embrace. As Rhoda looked on at Matt kissing the Spanish girl, she wistfully sighed, turned and grabbed the closest of the drunk Canadians, pulling Scott in for a snog. Within seconds, Rhoda released her grip on him before turning to Ryan and pulling him in for a kiss.

As the people around them began to break away from one another and continued to dance, Lola and Noodle remained planted to the spot, arms tight around each other. Looking in Noodle's eyes, she saw a rare glimmer of happiness and contentment, and hoped it would stay for longer this time, but knowing all too well that it may never properly return.

Watching Josh and Ambur disappear hand in hand into the thick crowd, Isabella looked at Matt with a knowing smile as she knew what their friends were up to.

'So amigo, what have *I* got to do to get *you* into bed?' Isabella said into Matt's ear, as they moved together in a sea of dancers.

'Asking nicely sometimes works, but you'll have to wait until tomorrow,' he replied, unsure whether she was serious or just testing him.

'*Tomorrow*? No, you'll lose your little bet and I don't think I could live with that on my conscience,' she said.

'Sorry, but I really can't,' Matt said as he stopped dancing and gave her a serious look in the eye.

'So you're turning me down?'

'Yep,' he smiled.

'What, even if I do this?' she asked, as her left hand slid down his stomach and between the waistband of his shorts causing him to jerk away from her.

'I'm sorry Issi, you'll really have to wait. I'm not that easy,' he smiled, thinking about what Kermit and Ben would have to say if they found out, realising for the first time that he really *didn't* care about the bet.

'Okay, well, just for the record, I would have sex with you tonight if you wanted to,' Isabella said.

'Noted... and for the record, I wouldn't tell my mates back home even if we did,' Matt said, as he took a step back and continued to dance.

As the first hours of the year passed, Noodle suggested they all head to Tallow, which as the most easterly beach in Australia, they would witness the first light of the year. So, the nine friends began their walk to the beach beyond the lighthouse, joined by hundreds of others with the same idea.

Arriving at the beach, they found the sand was already crowded. Handfuls of surfers could be seen bobbing in the dark water or getting ready to paddle out, eager to catch their first waves of the year. The stormy sky that had loomed over the ocean and had posed a continued threat to the party, had now gone, leaving a light scattering of small fluffy white clouds in its place, which proved to be perfect for the sunrise as they illuminated the deep shades of red, orange and gold across the morning horizon. During this ambient moment of tranquillity and beauty, a frustratingly sober Ryan decided it would be a good time for a group photo. He tried his best to get everyone to their blistered and weary feet with the intention of having the sunrise as a stimulating backdrop, but it was a losing battle, so he settled for a stranger's offer to take one of the whole gang sat down. The snapshot

157

went unnoticed by Lola, who'd already fallen asleep snugly under Noodle's arm, and caught Rhoda with an arm tightly around each of the two exhausted and sober Canadians, one of which she felt must be her Mr Right, she just wasn't quite sure which, or in fact which one was Ryan and which was Scott.

Watching with tired eyes, as Josh began to skin up a joint, Ambur found a helpless smile of affection break across her face. Just over a week before she'd been thinking that her pining after the young Californian was a lost cause. After the few months spent in an on-off relationship, he'd just upped and left one day, declaring he needed to head to Fiji for a visa, unsure if he'd be back, without even offering her an invitation to join him. She knew at the time, as she still did, that he wouldn't stick around Byron Bay forever, but in the past few weeks, she'd realised, after talking with Isabella, that she didn't really want to either.

'Josh?' Ambur asked as he went to light the spliff.

'Yeah babe.'

'Issi, Matt and I are all going to buy a van this week and drive it across to the west coast. We want to know if you fancy joining us?' she asked flashing Isabella a quick smile.

'*What?*' Matt asked, unsure if he'd heard right. If there was such a plan he certainly wasn't aware of it.

'Ssshh,' Isabella quietly hissed before pulling him in close and kissing him.

'*A van?*' Josh asked. 'To W.A., as in Margaret River? Perth? You're buying a van and driving to the west?' Josh said, as he tried to take in the information. 'Yeah, *why not?*' Then with a little thought he sat up and looked over at the Canadians. 'Hey guys, either of you want to buy my car?'

Eleven

Banging a fist down upon the roof of what was once Josh's car and home, I watched the Canadians drive away, with Rhoda sat in the back seat, all headed for Brisbane. As far as I could fathom Rhoda still didn't seem to know the truth about my past, although I suspected on the journey, with the amount she liked to talk, it was sure to come up. Knowing that I should have warned the Canadians, I smiled at the thought of the discussions that might arise from any revelations among them.

On the way back to Liquid Dreams, I passed the small internet café that I had previously emailed from and decided to take the opportunity to catch up on news from home and put the bet to rest once and for all.

Logging on, I found not only the usual emails from my mum and Kermit, but also another from Ben. Opening it up, I was hopeful as ever for some news of Christmas and New Year back home, even just a mention of a walk around the town, but all I got was ...*so Matt, how's the backpacking going? Time's up are you a legend or a loser?*

As I reread his words in my mind, I felt an urge to email him back and tell him that I had achieved the childish bet, using the photo that Ryan had emailed to confirm it with photographic evidence. They would never need to know that I'd failed, or even that I'd had the chance and turned it down, but as I began to write a reply, I let my hands do the talking and explained it as it was.

Hi Ben,

So, backpacking... After only a month what can I tell you? It's definitely not like it is in the movies. It's so much better and at the same time far worse. It would have been awesome to travel here with you, but I don't regret making this journey alone, I just hope you make the most of these next few months and get what you need for uni.

Am I legend or a loser? Good question, although I suspect you already know the answer, because if I wasn't already a legend among you all for daring to look beyond the familiar confines of the Flying Duck and out of town, then I guess I wasn't the friend I thought I was.

Did I win the bet? Who cares? I won something far better and I'm sending you photographic proof of that!

Take it easy mate, buddy, dude, amigo (you pick) and I'll see you in a year or two.
Matt.

Stepping back out into the bright sunshine and feeling the hot ground beneath my bare soles, I continued my walk back to Liquid Dreams, still with enough time to fit in a quick surf before I had to see a man about a van.

Printed in the United Kingdom by
Lightning Source UK Ltd., Milton Keynes
137363UK00001B/322-330/P